THE SHATTERED CROWN

RAVEN FONTAINE

Indie Pen Press
Seattle, Washington USA
IndiePenPress.com

Second Edition: October 2024

Paperback ISBN 979-8-9916530-5-3

CONTENTS

ONE
A KINGDOM OF SHADOWS

Lyra's breath caught in her throat as she pressed herself against the rough bark of an ancient oak tree. The cool night air carried the metallic clink of armor and the low murmur of voices. Vanguard patrol.

She closed her eyes and willed her racing heart to slow. Inside. Out. In. Out. The forest around her pulsed with life - a quiet symphony of rustling leaves and nocturnal creatures. But beneath it all, an undercurrent of discord, a discord in the melody of the land.

The voices grew louder. Lyra risked a glance around the tree trunk. Moonlight glinted off polished breastplates as four Vanguard soldiers marched along the forest path, their eyes scanning the shadows.

"Did you hear about the skirmish at Oakridge?" One of them asked, his voice barely above a whisper.

Another soldier grunted. "Stinking rebels. When will they learn?"

Lyra's fists clenched at her sides. The urge to leap out, to confront them, to make them see the truth of what the

Vanguard had done to Aethoria, shot through her veins like wildfire.

But she couldn't. Not yet. Not alone.

She forced herself to breathe, to hold still, to...

The energy within her swelled without warning. A familiar tingling sensation spread from her core to her fingertips. No. Not now!

Lyra bit her lip, tasting blood as she fought to contain the magic that threatened to burst forth. It had happened more often lately, this loss of control. As if the power within her was becoming too strong to contain.

One of the soldiers stopped and cocked his head. "You hear something?"

Lyra squeezed her eyes shut, focusing all her will on suppressing the magic. Sweat beaded her brow. Her whole body shook with the effort.

"Nah, probably a squirrel or something," another soldier replied. "Come on, let's finish the patrol. I'm freezing..."

A twig snapped under Lyra's foot.

She froze.

The soldiers fell silent.

"There!" One of them shouted. "Behind that tree!"

Lyra's eyes flew open. No more hiding. She spun away from the tree and sprinted deeper into the forest. Branches whipped at her face as she ran, her feet finding the uneven ground with practiced ease.

"Halt! In the name of the Vanguard!"

The cry was accompanied by the whistle of an arrow. It buried itself in a tree trunk inches from Lyra's head. She didn't slow down.

Her lungs burned as she pushed harder, faster. The sound of pursuit faded as she weaved through the trees, taking a path only she knew.

But the effort took its toll. The magic within her surged again, stronger this time. Lyra stumbled, barely catching herself against a tree. Her vision swam.

"No," she gasped. "Not here. Not now."

The air around her began to shimmer, leaves rustling without wind. She had to get away, had to...

A hand gripped her shoulder.

Lyra reacted on instinct. She twisted, her fist connecting with her attacker's jaw. There was a satisfying crunch and a cry of pain.

"Lyra! It's me!"

She blinked, her vision clearing. Aren stood in front of her, rubbing his jaw. His dark eyes were wide with worry.

"Aren?" Lyra's voice cracked. "What are you doing here?"

He grabbed her arm, already dragging her along. "Saving you, apparently. Come on, we have to move. The patrol-"

"This way!" A cry rang out behind them. Too close.

Aren swore under his breath. "Run!"

They sprinted through the forest, Aren leading the way. Lyra's breath came in ragged gasps, her legs burning with exhaustion. But she kept going, one foot in front of the other.

The sounds of the pursuit grew louder.

"We're not going to make it," Lyra panted.

Aren's grip on her arm tightened. "Yes, we are. Almost there."

They broke through a thick clump of bushes and skidded to a halt at the edge of a cliff. Far below, a river roared through a narrow gorge.

Lyra's eyes widened. "Aren, we can't--"

He turned to her, his expression grim. "Do you trust me?"

The shouts came closer. Any moment, the vanguard would break through the tree line.

Lyra met Aren's gaze and nodded once. "Always."

He gave her a tight smile. "Then jump."

Without hesitation, they leapt off the cliff just as the first soldier burst through the bushes. Lyra's stomach lurched as they plunged into the churning water below. The wind whipped at her hair, ripping the breath from her lungs.

And then they hit the water.

The shock of the cold drove the air from Lyra's lungs. For a moment, there was nothing but the roar of the current and the sting of the icy water. Then Aren's hand found hers and pulled her to the surface.

They gasped for air as the river carried them swiftly downstream, away from the shouts of the frustrated Vanguard soldiers.

"That was too close," Aren said between breaths.

Lyra nodded, unable to speak. The adrenaline was wearing off, leaving her exhausted and shaking. And as the immediate danger passed, the magic within her surged again.

She screamed as pain shot through her body. Blue light flickered around her hands, casting eerie shadows on the surface of the water.

Aren's eyes widened. "Lyra? What's happening?"

"I can't..." She gritted her teeth against another wave of pain. "I can't control it!"

The water around them began to churn, defying the natural flow of the river. Aren struggled to keep them both afloat as miniature whirlpools formed and dissipated around them.

"Lyra, you have to stop!"

"I'm trying!"

But the magic would not be contained. It built and built, a pressure in her chest that threatened to tear her apart. Lyra screamed as it finally broke free.

A shockwave of blue energy exploded outward. The river itself seemed to pause for a heartbeat before surging forward with renewed force. Aren and Lyra were swept under, tumbling in the suddenly violent current.

Lyra flailed, disoriented, lungs burning. Which way was up? Her vision began to darken at the edges. She was going to drown, she was-

Strong arms wrapped around her waist and pulled her up. They broke the surface again, Aren coughing and sputtering beside her.

"Hold on!" He shouted over the roar of the water. "I see a shore ahead!"

Lyra could only nod weakly as Aren guided her toward the shore. Her whole body felt like lead, the magic draining from her in a way she'd never experienced before.

With a final push, they dragged themselves to the muddy shore. Lyra collapsed onto her back, staring up at the star-filled sky as she gasped for air. Beside her, Aren did the same.

For a long moment, the only sound was their ragged breathing and the continued rush of the river.

Finally, Aren spoke. "What... what was that?"

Lyra shook her head, her voice barely above a whisper. "I don't know. It's getting worse, Aren. I can't control it anymore."

He propped himself up on one elbow and looked down at her with a mixture of concern and something else. Fear? "We have to get you back to camp. Thorne will know what to do."

Lyra nodded, but made no move to get up. Every muscle in her body cried out in protest at the mere thought of moving.

Aren's expression softened. He reached out and brushed a strand of wet hair from her face. "Rest for a moment. We're safe here for now."

She wanted to argue, to insist that they keep moving. But her eyelids were so heavy...

"Aren?" Lyra murmured, fighting to stay awake.

"Hmm?"

"Thank you. For coming back for me."

His hand found hers, squeezing gently. "Always, Lyra. I'll always come back for you."

As Lyra drifted off into an exhausted sleep, she couldn't shake the feeling that everything was about to change. The magic within her was growing stronger, more unpredictable. And somewhere out there, the Vanguard was hunting her.

The real battle was just beginning.

TWO
THE RELUCTANT MAGE

Darius stood atop the Shattered Spire, his gaze sweeping over the sprawling city of Solara below. The first light of dawn painted the sky with shades of pink and gold, but the beauty was lost on him. His fingers absently traced the Vanguard insignia on his chest as he wrestled with the uneasiness gnawing at his gut.

"Admiring the view, Darius?"

He turned to see Archmage Calidus approaching, his ornate robes billowing in the morning breeze. Darius straightened and offered a crisp bow. "Archmage. I didn't expect to see you up here so early."

Calidus' lips curled into a thin smile. "The burden of leadership, my boy. Our work never truly ends." He joined Darius at the parapet, his keen eyes scanning the horizon. "Beautiful, isn't it? A city at peace, protected by our power."

Darius nodded, not daring to speak. He'd seen the "peace" Calidus spoke of - the fear in people's eyes, the whispered conversations that stopped when a Vanguard mage passed.

"You seem troubled," Calidus said, his tone deceptively light. "Doubts about your new position?"

"No, Archmage," Darius replied quickly. Too quickly. He took a breath, calmed himself. "It is an honor to serve as your apprentice. I only hope I can live up to your expectations."

Calidus patted him on the shoulder. "You have already surpassed them, Darius. Your talents are... extraordinary. Which is why I have a special task for you."

Darius' pulse quickened. "What kind of task?"

The Archmage's eyes hardened. "We have received reports of increased rebel activity in the Eastern Forests. I want you to lead a team to investigate and... deal with the situation."

"Deal with it?" Darius echoed, his mouth suddenly dry.

"By any means necessary," Calidus said, his voice cold. "These rebels threaten everything we have built. They must be stopped, Darius. Permanently."

Darius swallowed hard, forcing his face to remain impassive. "I understand, Archmage. When do we leave?"

"Immediately. Captain Roderick and his men are waiting for you in the courtyard." Calidus turned to leave, then paused. "Oh, and Darius? There are whispers of a powerful mage among the rebels. If you find her... bring her to me. Alive."

With that, the Archmage swept away, leaving Darius alone with the weight of his orders. He closed his eyes and took a shaky breath. This was what he had trained for, what he had worked so hard for. So why did it feel so wrong?

No time for doubts now. He had a job to do.

The Eastern Forests loomed before them, a sea of green stretching to the horizon. Darius sat on his horse, flanked by Captain Roderick and a dozen Vanguard soldiers. They had been riding for days, following reports of rebel sightings.

"Mage Darius," Roderick called, his gruff voice cutting through Darius' thoughts. "We should make camp soon. The men need rest, and these woods aren't safe after dark."

Darius nodded, scanning the tree line. "Agreed. There's a clearing ahead. We'll set up there and..."

A scream pierced the air, followed by the clash of steel on steel.

"Ambush!" Roderick roared, drawing his sword.

Chaos erupted around them. Rebels poured from the trees, engaging the Vanguard soldiers in fierce battle. Darius leapt from his horse, magic crackling at his fingertips. He fired a bolt of energy at the nearest attacker, sending them flying backward.

"Protect the mage!" Roderick shouted, cutting down a rebel with a ferocious blow.

Darius spun, deflecting an arrow with a hastily erected energy shield. His training took over, muscle memory guiding his movements as he wove spells of protection and attack. But for every rebel they struck down, two more seemed to take their place.

A flash of movement caught his eye. A figure darted through the trees, heading deeper into the forest. Something about their fluid grace, the way they moved...

"The rebel leader," Darius breathed. Without thinking, he took off in pursuit.

"Darius, wait!" Roderick's voice faded behind him as Darius plunged into the forest.

He ran, ducking under low-hanging branches and leaping over fallen logs. The figure ahead was fast, but Darius was driven by something more than duty. A need to understand, to see the face of the one who dared to defy the vanguard.

The trees thinned, opening into a small clearing. Darius burst through the foliage, magic blazing in his hands - and froze.

A young woman stood before him, her chest heaving with effort. Her dark hair was pulled back in a messy braid, and her clothes were worn and patched. But it was her eyes that captured Darius. Fierce and defiant, they blazed with an inner fire that took his breath away.

For a moment, neither moved. The sounds of battle faded to a distant rumble.

"Well?" The woman said, breaking the silence. "Are you going to attack me or not?"

Darius blinked, off balance. This was not how he had imagined a confrontation with a rebel leader. "I... who are you?"

She raised an eyebrow. "Shouldn't you know by now? Or does the Vanguard make a habit of going after people they can't identify?"

Despite himself, Darius felt the corner of his mouth twitch. "I'm Darius," he said, lowering his hands slightly. "And you are...?"

"Going," she replied with a wry smile. She took a step back, toward the trees.

"Wait!" Darius called. "I can't let you go. You're... you're under arrest, in the name of the Vanguard."

The woman's eyes narrowed. "And if I refuse?"

Darius raised his hands, magic shimmering around them. "Please don't make this difficult. I don't want to hurt you."

"Funny," she said, her own hands beginning to glow with power. "I was going to say the same thing."

The air crackled with tension. Darius' heart raced, but not with fear. There was something about this woman, something calling to him on a level he couldn't explain.

"Stand down," he said, but the words lacked conviction. "This doesn't have to end in violence."

Her lips curled into a sad smile. "It always ends in violence with the Vanguard. You should know that better than anyone, *mage*."

The way she spat out the word stung more than Darius expected. "You don't know me," he said softly.

"And you don't know us," she shot back. "You don't know what the Vanguard has done, what they continue to do to innocent people. But you could."

Darius frowned. "What do you mean?"

She took a step forward, her eyes never leaving his. "Join us, Darius. Help us fight for true peace, not this mockery of order the Vanguard imposes."

For a wild moment, Darius considered. The doubts he'd harbored, the discomfort with the Vanguard's methods... But no. He couldn't betray everything he had worked for, everything he believed in. Could he?

"I... I can't," he said, his voice barely above a whisper.

The woman nodded, as if she'd expected his answer. "Then I'm sorry."

Before Darius could react, she thrust her hands forward. A wave of pure magical energy hit him, sending him flying backwards. He hit a tree hard, his vision blurring as he crashed to the ground.

Through the haze of pain, he saw the woman approach. She knelt beside him, her expression a mixture of remorse and determination.

"My name is Lyra," she said softly. "Remember this, Darius. Remember this moment. And when you're ready to see the truth, find us."

With that, she was gone, disappearing into the shadows of the forest. Darius tried to call out, to move, but darkness crept into the edges of his vision. As he slipped into unconsciousness, a thought echoed in his mind.

Lyra. Her name was Lyra.

The last thing he heard before the darkness took him was Captain Roderick's voice calling his name in the distance. But it was Lyra's face he saw as he drifted away, her eyes burning with a fire that would haunt his dreams for days to come.

THREE
WHISPERS OF POWER

Lyra's muscles screamed in protest as she dragged herself over the crumbling stone wall. The rebel camp sprawled before her, a patchwork of tents and makeshift structures nestled in the heart of Whispering Grove. She paused, taking in the familiar sights and sounds-the clang of a blacksmith's hammer, the aroma of stew wafting from the communal kitchen, the laughter of children playing between the tents.

Home. At least for now.

"Lyra!"

She turned to see Mira sprinting toward her, the young mage's face aglow with relief. "You're back! We were so worried when-" Mira skidded to a halt, her eyes wide. "You look terrible."

Lyra managed a weak smile. "Thanks. You really know how to make a girl feel special."

Mira flushed. "I didn't mean-I'm sorry, I-"

"It's okay," Lyra said, squeezing the younger girl's shoulder. "I've had a rough couple of days. Is Thorne around? I need to talk to him. Urgently."

Mira nodded, her expression becoming serious. "He's in the strategy tent. But Lyra, what happened out there? The others came back days ago, said you and Aren got separated during the ambush."

Lyra's mind flashed back to the vanguard mage, Darius. His piercing eyes, the conflict she'd sensed in him. She shook her head, pushing the memory aside. "It's... complicated. I'll explain later. Right now, I need to..."

"Lyra!"

Aren's voice boomed across the camp. He strode toward them, his face a storm of relief and anger. "Where in the name of the Old Gods have you been? I've had search parties combing the forest for days!"

Lyra winced. "I'm sorry, Aren. After we got separated at the river, I had to lay low for a while. There were Vanguard patrols everywhere."

Aren's expression softened slightly. He reached out and pulled her into a brief, violent embrace. "I'm glad you're safe," he murmured. Then he pulled back, his eyes narrowing. "But don't ever do anything like this again. Do you hear me? I thought..." His voice trailed off. "We thought we'd lost you."

The guilt hit Lyra like a physical blow. She had been so focused on her own struggles, on the growing chaos of her powers, that she hadn't stopped to consider how her disappearance would affect the others. "I'm sorry," she said again, meaning it. "It won't happen again."

Aren nodded, some of the tension leaving his shoulders.

"Make sure it doesn't. Now, what's this about needing to see Thorne?"

Lyra hesitated. How could she explain what had happened at the river? The surge of power she couldn't control, the way it had changed the flow of the water itself? "I... I need his guidance," she said finally. "Something is happening to me, Aren. To my magic. And I'm afraid."

Aren's eyebrows shot up. In all the years they'd known each other, Lyra had never admitted to being afraid of anything. He exchanged a look with Mira, then nodded. "Alright. Let's go see the old man."

The strategy tent was a mess of maps, scrolls, and glowing crystals. Thorne was hunched over a table in the center, his weathered hands tracing lines on a large map of Aethoria. He looked up as they entered, his bushy eyebrows raised at the sight of Lyra.

"So the prodigal daughter returns," he said, his gruff voice tinged with relief. "I was beginning to think we'd have to storm the Shattered Spire itself to get you back."

Lyra managed a weak smile. "It would take more than a few Vanguard thugs to keep me away."

Thorne grunted, but his eyes twinkled with amusement. "Well, don't just stand there gawking. Sit down before you fall over. You look like you've been dragged backwards through the Veiled Mountains."

Lyra sank gratefully into a chair, flanked by Aren and Mira. Thorne poured a cup of steaming liquid from a pot over the fire and pressed it into her hands. She inhaled deeply, the familiar scent of herbs and spices soothing her frayed nerves.

"Now," Thorne said, settling into his own chair. "Tell me what troubles you, child."

Lyra took a deep breath and began to speak. She told them everything-the chase through the forest, the uncontrollable surge of power at the river, her encounter with the Vanguard mage. As she spoke, Thorne's expression grew increasingly serious.

When she finished, the tent fell silent. Aren paced restlessly, while Mira stared at Lyra with a mixture of awe and concern.

Finally, Thorne spoke. "I was afraid this would happen," he said quietly.

Lyra leaned forward. "What do you mean? Do you know what's happening to me?"

Thorne sighed heavily. "Your power is growing, Lyra. Faster than I expected. The royal bloodline has always carried strong magic, but in you..." He shook his head. "In you, it's something else entirely."

"But why now?" Aren demanded. "Why is she suddenly going crazy?"

"Because it's coming into its full potential," Thorne replied. "The magic of the land itself is responding to her. It's... awakening."

Lyra's head spun. "I don't understand. How can I have so much power? I'm not special, I'm-"

"You are the rightful heir to the throne of Aethoria," Thorne interrupted, his voice sharp. "The last of the Valenwood line. Your parents-" He trailed off, pain flickering across his face. "Your parents knew this day would come. They prepared for it as best they could."

Lyra's breath caught in her throat. Her parents. She had only dim memories of them - her father's warm laugh, her mother's gentle hands. They'd died when she was young, killed in the Vanguard coup. Or so she'd always believed.

"What do you mean they were preparing?" she whispered.

Thorne stood and walked to a chest in the corner of the tent. He rummaged inside for a moment before returning with a small, ornate box. "This was entrusted to me by your mother on the night of the attack. She made me swear to keep it safe until you were ready."

With shaking hands, Lyra took the box. It hummed with energy, responding to her touch. She opened it slowly, revealing a delicate silver circle resting on a bed of velvet. In its center, a blue gem pulsated with an inner light.

"The Crown of Whispers," Thorne said quietly. "It's been in your family for generations. A channel for royal magic, and a symbol of the true ruler of Aethoria."

Lyra stared at the circlet, her mind reeling. All her life she'd thought of herself as nothing more than a rebel, fighting against the oppression of the Vanguard. But this... this changed everything.

"I can't," she said, her voice barely above a whisper. "I can't be what you say I am. I'm not a ruler, I'm not-"

"You are exactly what you were born to be," Thorne said firmly. He knelt in front of her and took her hands in his. "Lyra, listen to me. True power comes from within, not from controlling others. The Vanguard never understood that. But you... you have the potential to bring balance back to our land. To heal the wounds the Vanguard has inflicted."

Lyra met his gaze and saw the unwavering faith in his eyes.

She glanced at Aren, who nodded solemnly, and at Mira, whose face glowed with hope.

Slowly, hesitantly, Lyra reached for the circle. The moment her fingers touched the cool metal, a surge of energy went through her. The jewel came to life, bathing the tent in blue light. Lyra gasped as knowledge flooded her mind - centuries of history, the deep magic of the land, secrets long forgotten.

As the light faded, Lyra blinked, her vision clearing. The others stared at her in awe.

"Well," Aren said, breaking the silence. "I guess that settles it. Hail Queen Lyra, rightful ruler of Aethoria."

Lyra shot him a look. "Don't you dare start bowing."

A grin tugged at Aren's lips. "Wouldn't dream of it, Your Majesty."

Despite everything, Lyra found herself smiling. But as the weight of the circlet settled on her forehead, so did the weight of responsibility. She thought of the Vanguard, of the suffering they had caused her people. Of Darius and the conflict she'd seen in his eyes.

"What do we do now?" she asked, looking at Thorne.

The old man's eyes glowed with a mixture of pride and determination. "Now, my dear, we prepare for war. The Vanguard will not surrender its power without a fight. And we have much to teach you about your heritage, about the true nature of your magic."

Lyra nodded and squared her shoulders. Whatever challenges lay ahead, she would face them. For her parents, for her people, for the future of Aethoria.

As if in response to her resolve, the gem in the circlet pulsed once more. Lyra's eyes widened as a vision flashed before her

- a great battle, magic tearing the sky asunder, and at the center of it all, a figure wrapped in blue flame.

The vision faded as quickly as it had come, leaving Lyra breathless. She looked up to find the others watching her with concern.

"Lyra?" Mira asked hesitantly. "Are you all right?"

Lyra opened her mouth to answer, but before she could speak, a commotion broke out outside the tent. Shouts of alarm rang out, followed by the clash of steel on steel.

Aren was on his feet in an instant, sword in hand. "We're under attack!"

As they rushed out of the tent, Lyra's mind raced. The Vanguard couldn't have found them, not here in the heart of the Whispering Grove. Unless...

Unless they'd been betrayed.

The thought chilled her to the bone as she stepped out into the chaos, the future she'd glimpsed in her vision suddenly seeming much closer than she'd ever imagined.

FOUR
THE FIST OF THE VANGUARD

The village of Oakridge nestled in the foothills of the Veiled Mountains, a haven of thatched roofs and weathered stone. As dawn broke, wisps of smoke curled from the chimneys, and the smell of baking bread wafted through the narrow streets.

Darius stood at the edge of the forest and watched. His hands clenched and unclenched at his sides, a war raging within him.

"Orders, sir?" Captain Roderick's harsh voice cut through his thoughts.

Darius turned to face the assembled Vanguard troops. Two dozen men, armed to the teeth, ready to descend upon an unsuspecting village. His village.

"Remember," Darius said, his voice steady despite the churning in his stomach, "we are here to root out rebel sympathizers. No unnecessary violence."

Roderick's lip curled. "With all due respect, sir, Archmage Calidus was clear. We're here to make an example of this place."

Darius met the captain's gaze, unflinching. "And we will. But we will do it my way. Understand?"

A tense moment passed before Roderick nodded, reluctance etched into every line of his face. "As you say, sir."

Darius turned back to the village, his childhood home. He'd dreamed of returning as a hero, of using his position in the Vanguard to make things better. Now he returned a conqueror.

He raised his hand, magic shimmering around his fingers. "Move out."

The Vanguard troops surged forward, a tide of steel and purpose. As they reached the edge of the village, Darius unleashed a bolt of energy into the sky. It exploded with a thunderous crack, sending birds scattering from the trees.

Chaos ensued. Villagers poured from their homes, eyes wide with fear as they took in the approaching soldiers. Screams filled the air, along with the sound of shattering pottery and splintering wood as people scrambled to flee or hide.

"Round them up!" Roderick shouted. "Search every house, every cellar!"

Darius strode through the village square, his mere presence enough to send people scurrying out of his way. He tried to ignore the familiar faces, the looks of betrayal and horror cast in his direction.

A commotion to his left caught his attention. Two Vanguard soldiers were dragging an old man from his home, the elder's feet barely touching the ground.

"Please," the old man gasped, "I have done nothing wrong!"

Darius's blood ran cold as he recognized the voice. Old Finnian, the village herbalist. The man who'd tended to Darius' childhood scrapes and fevers.

"Sir!" One of the soldiers called. "We found rebel propaganda in his house. What do we do with him?"

Finnian's rheumy eyes found Darius and widened in recognition. "Little Dari? Is that you, boy?"

Darius jumped at the childhood nickname. He opened his mouth to reply, but Roderick's voice cut through the square.

"Burn it," the captain ordered. "Burn it all. Let them see what happens to those who defy the Vanguard."

"No!" The cry tore from Darius' throat before he could stop it. He whirled at Roderick. "I said no unnecessary violence. We question them, we don't--"

A woman's scream pierced the air, followed by a child's terrified wail. Darius spun to see flames licking up the side of a house, a Vanguard soldier standing in front of it, torch in hand.

"Stop!" Darius yelled, magic flaring around him. "I order you to-"

An explosion shook the square. Darius stumbled, almost losing his footing. As the dust settled, he saw a group of figures emerge from the shadows between the buildings. Rebels.

"Protect the villagers!" A familiar voice rang out. Lyra.

She stood atop an overturned wagon, her dark hair whipping in the wind. The Crown of Whispers glittered on her forehead, pulsing with blue light.

Their eyes met across the chaos, and for a moment, the world fell away. Darius saw the pain in her gaze, the determination. She saw his conflict, his shame.

Then the moment shattered as Roderick's voice cut through the din. "It's the rebel leader! Take her down!"

Arrows whistled through the air. Darius moved without thinking, creating a magical barrier around Lyra. The arrows rattled harmlessly to the ground.

Lyra's eyes widened in surprise, but she wasted no time. With a gesture, she sent a wave of power through the square, knocking the Vanguard soldiers off their feet.

Battle broke out in earnest. Rebels clashed with Vanguard troops, steel clashing against steel. Villagers caught in the middle ran for cover or joined the fray, armed with whatever they could find.

Darius found himself in the eye of the storm, fending off attacks from both sides. He spotted old Finnian crouching behind a barrel and rushed to the old man's side.

"Finnian," he said urgently, "you need to get out of here. Take as many people as you can and head for the caves in the foothills."

The herbalist looked up at him, confusion and fear warring in his wrinkled face. "Dari, what's going on? Why are you with these monsters?"

The words stung more than any physical blow. Darius swallowed hard. "I'm sorry," he whispered. "I thought... I thought I was doing the right thing. But this?" He gestured to the chaos around them. "This isn't right. Please, go. I'll try to buy you some time."

Finnian hesitated, then nodded. He scurried away, gathering a group of villagers as he went.

Darius turned back to the battle, his resolve hardening. He might not be able to undo the damage he'd done, but he could try to mitigate it.

He weaved his way through the fighting, using his magic to create barriers between the Vanguard soldiers and the fleeing villagers. One rebel charged at him, sword raised, but Darius simply dodged, pushing the man toward a group of fleeing children.

"Protect them!" He shouted over the din.

The rebel blinked in confusion, but didn't hesitate to lead the children to safety.

Across the square, Lyra was a whirlwind of movement. Her magic pulsed with every movement, sending Vanguard soldiers flying. But Darius could see the strain on her face, the way her hands trembled.

He fought his way toward her, using his power to clear a path. As he approached, he saw Roderick approaching from her blind side, sword raised for a killing blow.

"Lyra!" Darius yelled. "Behind you!"

She turned, but too slowly. Darius lunged forward, throwing up a barrier. Roderick's sword struck it, the impact sending shockwaves through Darius' body.

Lyra stared at him, her eyes wide with surprise and something else. Understanding? Before either of them could speak, a fresh wave of Vanguard reinforcements poured into the square.

"We have to go!" Aren's voice broke through the chaos. He appeared at Lyra's side, bloodied but standing tall. "Lyra, we can't hold them off much longer!"

She nodded, her eyes still locked with Darius'. "What about the villagers?"

"Most have fled to the hills," Darius said quickly. "I'll... I'll make sure the rest get to safety."

Lyra's brow furrowed. "Why are you helping us?"

A thousand answers flashed through Darius' mind. Because it's right. Because I can't stand by and watch innocent people suffer. Because something about you makes me question everything I thought I knew.

In the end, he simply said, "Because I have to."

For a heartbeat, neither moved. Then Lyra nodded, a silent acknowledgment passing between them.

"Aren," she said, her eyes never leaving Darius, "get our people out. I'll cover our retreat."

Aren looked between them, suspicion clear on his face. But he didn't argue, he was already shouting orders to the other rebels.

"This isn't over," Lyra told Darius, her voice deep and intense. "What the Vanguard is doing... it has to stop."

"I know," Darius replied, surprising himself with the conviction in his voice.

The ghost of a smile touched Lyra's lips. Then she turned and raised her hands. The air around her shimmered, and suddenly the square was filled with duplicates of the rebels, illusory copies that moved and fought like the real thing.

In the confusion, the rebels slipped away, taking as many villagers with them as they could. Darius watched them go, his heart pounding in his chest.

"Traitors!"

Roderick's angry roar snapped Darius back to reality. He turned to see the captain charging toward him, his face contorted with rage.

Darius raised his hands, magic crackling between his fingers. As Roderick's sword swung down, Darius made his choice.

The explosion of power sent both men flying in opposite directions. Darius hit the ground hard, his head swimming. Through the ringing in his ears, he heard shouts of confusion and alarm from the Vanguard soldiers.

He staggered to his feet, knowing he had only moments before they regrouped. His eyes scanned the square, taking in the destruction, the wounded, the remnants of the life he had once known.

There was no turning back now.

With a final burst of power, Darius shrouded himself in a veil of magic. To the Vanguard soldiers, it would appear as if he had vanished into thin air.

As he slipped into the forest, following the path the rebels had taken, a thought echoed through his mind:

What have I done?

The answer, he realized, was both simple and terrifying.

He had chosen a side.

FIVE

UNEASY ALLIANCES

Lyra's boots crunched in the mud as she led the ragtag group of rebels and villagers through the dense forest. The Whispering Grove lived up to its name, the leaves rustling with secrets as they passed. Behind them, she could hear the labored breathing of the injured and the muffled sobs of those who had lost everything.

"We have to stop," Aren said, falling into step beside her. His face was streaked with dirt and blood, his usually pristine hair plastered to his forehead. "The villagers can't keep up this pace."

Lyra nodded and scanned the area. Her eyes fell on a small clearing ahead, partially hidden by a cluster of ancient oaks. "There. We'll rest and regroup."

As they entered the clearing, Lyra's mind raced. The attack on Oakridge had been a disaster, but they'd saved as many as they could. And then there was Darius...

"All right, listen up," Lyra called, her voice cutting through the murmur of exhausted voices. "We'll rest here for an hour, no more. Mira, tend to the wounded. Aren, organize a perimeter guard. The rest of you, eat and rest while you can."

As the group dispersed, Lyra slumped against a tree, the weight of the Crown of Whispers suddenly heavy on her forehead. She closed her eyes and tried to center herself.

"You did well back there."

Lyra's eyes snapped open. Thorne stood before her, his weathered face etched with concern.

"Did I?" Lyra asked, bitterness creeping into her voice. "We barely escaped. Half the village burned. And for what? To prove to the Vanguard how dangerous we are?"

Thorne's gnarled hand rested on her shoulder. "You saved lives today, child. Never doubt that."

Lyra opened her mouth to reply, but a commotion at the edge of the clearing cut her off. Her heart leapt into her throat as she saw the cause.

Darius stumbled into view, aided by two rebel scouts. His Vanguard uniform was torn and bloodied, his face pale under a layer of dirt.

"We found him following our trail," one of the scouts reported. "Says he wants to help."

In an instant, the clearing erupted into chaos. Villagers recoiled in fear, while rebels grabbed for weapons. Aren was there in a heartbeat, sword drawn and pointed at Darius' throat.

"Give me one reason why I shouldn't finish you right here," Aren growled.

Darius didn't flinch. His eyes found Lyra's across the clearing. "Because she knows I'm not her enemy."

Silence fell over the group. All eyes were on Lyra, waiting for her decision. She felt the weight of their expectation, their fear, their hope.

"Lower your weapon, Aren," she said, her voice calm despite the turmoil in her stomach.

Aren's head whipped around, disbelief etched into his features. "You can't be serious. He's Vanguard! He led the attack on Oakridge!"

"And he saved my life," Lyra countered. She stepped forward and addressed the group. "He helped the villagers escape. He turned against his own people to protect us."

Murmurs rippled through the crowd. Lyra saw confusion, anger, and a glimmer of hope on several faces.

"It could be a trick," Aren pointed out. "He could be leading the Vanguard right to us."

Darius straightened, wincing. "If I wanted you dead, I wouldn't have warned Lyra about the ambush. I wouldn't have let you escape."

"Why should we believe you?" This from old Finnian, the village herbalist. His rheumy eyes were sharp with suspicion.

Darius' shoulders slumped. "Because I've seen the truth of what the Vanguard has become. What I've become." His voice cracked. "I joined to protect people, not... not this. Not slaughtering innocent villagers and burning homes."

A tense silence fell over the clearing. Lyra could almost feel the scales tipping, the fragile balance of trust and suspicion.

"Lyra," Aren said, his voice deep and urgent. "You can't seriously be considering this. He's dangerous. He's-"

"He's our best chance to understand the Vanguard's plans," Lyra cut him off. She met Darius' gaze, saw the pain and determination there. "And I think he may be our best chance to stop them."

More murmurs, some angry, some pensive. Lyra raised her voice, addressing the entire group. "I know you're afraid. I know you've lost much. But this war will not be won with hate alone. If we turn away everyone who has ever made a mistake, who has ever been on the wrong side, how can we hope to change anything?"

She moved to stand in front of Darius, close enough to see the gold flecks in his green eyes. "I believe him. I believe he wants to help. And I'm willing to give him that chance."

For a moment, no one moved. Then, slowly, the old Finnian stepped forward. He looked up at Darius, his face a map of wrinkles and hard-won wisdom.

"You've always been a good boy, Dari," he said quietly. "A little too eager to please, but your heart was in the right place." He turned to Lyra. "If you trust him, my lady, then so do I."

It was as if a dam had burst. Villagers and rebels alike began to voice their support, some grudgingly, others with growing hope. Aren's sword wavered, then fell.

"If you're wrong about this," he muttered to Lyra, "it could destroy everything we've built."

Lyra nodded, the weight of her decision settling on her shoulders. "I know. But if I'm right, it could save us all."

As the crowd dispersed, Lyra turned back to Darius. He swayed on his feet, exhaustion evident in every line of his body.

"Thank you," he said, his voice barely above a whisper.

Lyra's hand moved of its own accord, brushing a strand of hair from his forehead. She felt a jolt of... something pass between them at the contact. "Don't make me regret this," she said softly.

The ghost of a smile touched Darius' lips. "I won't. I promise."

As Mira led Darius away to tend to his wounds, Lyra found herself watching him go. The connection between them was undeniable, a pull she couldn't quite explain. It thrilled and terrified her in equal measure.

"You play a dangerous game, child."

Lyra turned to find Thorne at her elbow, his eyes sharp under bushy eyebrows.

"I'm doing what I think is right," she replied.

Thorne nodded slowly. "As you must. But be careful. The heart can be a treacherous thing, especially in wartime."

Before Lyra could answer, a call came from the edge of the clearing.

"Vanguard patrol! This way!"

In an instant, the relative calm of the camp was shattered. Lyra's mind raced. They weren't ready for another fight, not with so many injured and exhausted.

Her eyes met Darius' across the clearing. In that moment, she saw her own fear and determination reflected in his gaze.

"Everyone, stay calm," Lyra called, her voice steadier than she felt. "Aren, get the villagers ready. Mira, help the wounded. Darius..."

She hesitated, aware of the weight of everyone's eyes.

Darius straightened, squaring his shoulders despite his injuries. "I can create a diversion. Buy you time to escape."

Aren's eyes narrowed. "And lead them right to us? I don't think so."

"No," Lyra said, an idea forming. "Not a diversion. A deception." She turned to Darius. "Your Vanguard uniform. Put it back on."

Understanding dawned in Darius' eyes. "You want me to lead them astray."

Lyra nodded. "Can you do it?"

For a moment, Darius hesitated. Lyra saw the conflict in his eyes, the last vestiges of loyalty struggling with his newfound resolve.

Then he straightened, meeting her gaze with a determination that sent a shiver down her spine. "For you? Anything."

As the group scrambled to prepare, Lyra felt the familiar surge of magic within her. But this time, it wasn't the chaotic force she'd struggled with before. It was a steady warmth, pulsing in time with her heartbeat.

She caught Darius' eye as he pulled on his torn Vanguard cloak. Something passed between them, unspoken but powerful.

Trust. Hope. And something more, something neither of them dared to name.

As Darius strode toward the oncoming patrol, back straight and head held high, Lyra allowed herself a moment of doubt. Had she made the right decision? Could she really trust a man who had been her enemy only hours before?

But as she watched him leave, the last rays of sunlight glinting off his Vanguard insignia, she knew in her heart that everything had changed.

For better or worse, their fates were now intertwined.

The real question was: where would this new path take them?

And would Aethoria survive the journey?

SIX
RESCUE AND SACRIFICE

The Shattered Spire pierced the night sky like a broken blade, its twisted architecture an affront to the natural order. Darius pressed himself against the weathered stone, counting heartbeats as he waited for the patrol to pass. It had been three hours since the prisoners had escaped, three hours since their spy had revealed Lyra's location in this maze of corrupted stone and dark magic.

"Our contact's information better be good," Aren whispered, fingers drumming silently against his sword hilt. "We lost six good people tracking down those escaped prisoners."

"It's good." Darius had interrogated the captured Vanguard messenger himself. The man's fear had been genuine - as had his desire to atone for serving Calidus. "Lyra's being held in the upper chambers. They're preparing some kind of ritual."

Mira nodded, her young face drawn with exhaustion from hours of magical probing. "The stations are weakest on the eastern wall. If we're going to break through..." She trailed off, glancing at the hastily assembled rescue team—eight of their best - all that could be gathered in the chaos following the prison break.

"The timeline?" Aren asked.

"Dawn." Darius's jaw clenched. "Whatever they're planning, it happens at dawn."

Beside him, Aren's fingers drummed silently against his sword hilt – an old soldier's tell.

"The eastern wall," Mira whispered, her voice barely stirring the air. "The stations are weakest there. If we're going to break through..." She trailed off, young face drawn with exhaustion from hours of magical probing.

Darius nodded, throat tight. Somewhere in that maze of corrupted stone and dark magic, Lyra waited. And with her, their unborn child – a beacon of power that Calidus would twist to his own ends if given the chance.

"This is madness," Aren muttered, eyes scanning the battlements above. "The Spire's defenses—"

"Are formidable," Darius cut him off. "But not impenetrable. Not anymore." His hand unconsciously touched the spot where the Vanguard insignia had once rested. "I helped design them, remember?"

The ghost of a smile touched Aren's lips. "And now you'll help us break them. The irony would be delicious if we weren't all about to die."

"Save the gallows humor for after we've rescued your queen." Darius turned to the small team of rebels crouched in the shadows. Eight of their best – though 'best' was relative when most were farmers and craftsmen who'd learned war by necessity. "Remember: we move fast, we move quiet, and we don't stop until we reach Lyra. Clear?"

A series of nods answered him. Their eyes held a mix of fear and determination that made his chest ache. These were

Lyra's people, willing to die for their queen – and for him, a former enemy who'd earned their trust one bloody battle at a time.

Darius reached for his magic, feeling it respond sluggishly. Weeks of constant fighting had left him drained, but he'd have to make do. They all would.

"On my mark," he breathed, gathering what power he could. The familiar tingle of magic built beneath his skin, different now than in his Vanguard days. Less controlled, more alive. "Three... two... one..."

He thrust his hands forward, channeling everything he had into a focused burst of energy. The stations flared to life, ancient wards struggling to repel his attack. Darius gritted his teeth, pushing harder. Sweat beaded on his forehead as he grappled with defenses he himself had once strengthened.

For a moment, nothing happened. Then, with a sound like shattering glass, a section of the magical barrier collapsed.

"Now!"

They surged forward as one, Aren taking point with blade drawn. The first wave of guards never saw them coming – precision strikes dropped them before they could raise the alarm. But it wouldn't last. It couldn't.

Alarms wailed as they fought their way deeper into the Spire. Darius moved on instinct, magic, and martial training, combining in lethal efficiency. A guard's sword thrust became an opening for a blast of force. A magical attack deflected into another opponent's path. But for every foe they dropped, two more seemed to appear.

"This way!" Mira called her magical senses, guiding them through twisting corridors. Her gift for tracking magical signatures had proven invaluable since joining the rebellion. Now, it might mean the difference between success and failure.

They rounded a corner and ran straight into a squad of elite Vanguard mages. The air crackled as spells flew, raw power meeting trained precision in a deadly dance. Darius deflected a bolt of lightning, feeling the residual energy skitter across his skin. On his left, Aren's blade sang as it cut through magical barriers.

But they were outnumbered, and fatigue was taking its toll. Darius saw one of the rebels go down, then another. Their tight formation began to fragment.

"Fall back!" he ordered, throwing up a shield to cover their retreat. "Mira, find us another route!"

The young mage closed her eyes, reaching out with her gift. "Service tunnel, two levels down," she reported after a moment. "It should lead us to the central chambers."

They fought their way to a narrow stairwell, the sounds of pursuit echoing too close behind. Darius brought up the rear, maintaining a barrier against the worst of the Vanguard's attacks. His magic felt stretched thin, like a rope about to snap.

Pain lanced through his side – a shard of pure energy piercing his guard. He stumbled, tasting copper.

"Darius!" Aren's grip on his arm kept him from falling. "You're hit!"

"Keep moving," Darius growled, forcing himself forward. The wound burned with each step, but he couldn't stop. Not now. Not when they were so close.

They reached a heavy stone door that practically hummed

with magical energy. Mira pressed her hand against it, brow furrowed in concentration.

"She's close," the young mage whispered. "I can feel her magic. But there's something else. Something... wrong."

Darius nodded grimly. "Calidus. Everyone be ready – this could get ugly."

With a combined effort, they forced the door open. The scene that greeted them stole the breath from Darius's lungs.

Lyra stood in the center of a vast chamber, wreathed in blinding blue light. The Crown of Whispers blazed on her forehead, its power visibly intertwined with something else – the raw, untamed magic of their unborn child. Before her, driven to his knees, knelt Archmage Calidus himself.

"Impossible," the Archmage gasped, face twisted with equal parts awe and terror.

Lyra's eyes found Darius, recognition and relief flooding her features. "Darius," she breathed, and in that single word, he heard everything they'd left unsaid.

The moment shattered as Calidus seized his chance. The Archmage moved with desperate speed, dark magic coalescing around his hands. Lyra stumbled, her concentration broken.

"No!" The cry tore from Darius's throat as he launched himself forward, ignoring the searing pain in his side. Time seemed to slow as he saw Calidus gather power for a killing strike. He saw the fear in Lyra's eyes, her hands moving to protect her stomach. And he saw the path he must take.

Without hesitation, Darius threw himself between Lyra and certain death. Calidus's spell struck him square in the chest, the impact lifting him off his feet. He had just enough time to meet Lyra's eyes, to try to form words that wouldn't come before darkness claimed him.

The impact sent him flying back into the far wall, and pain exploded through every nerve in his body. Through his darkening vision, he saw Lyra scream and felt the surge of her magic as she fought back against Calidus. He tried to call her name, to tell her everything he'd never said, but darkness claimed him before the words could form.

The last thing he heard was chaos erupting around him - shouts of alarm, the clash of steel, and beneath it all, a sound like reality tearing at the seams. Then nothing.

CONSCIOUSNESS RETURNED IN FRAGMENTS. There was pain. Voices argued nearby. There was the smell of healing herbs and something else—ozone, the aftermath of powerful magic.

"He's stabilizing," Mira's voice seemed to come from very far away. "But the magical backlash... I've never seen anything like it."

"Save your strength." That was Aren, sounding exhausted. "Focus on keeping him alive. The Queen will need him when she wakes."

Darius tried to ask about Lyra to understand what had happened after he had fallen, but his body refused to respond. Darkness pulled at him again.

The last thing he felt was a gentle hand on his forehead and a whispered promise: "Rest now. We'll be here when you wake."

Then oblivion claimed him once more, carrying him into dreams of blue fire and a crown that whispered of destiny.

His last thought was of her face – fierce, beautiful, and forever out of reach. Of the child they'd made together, the future they'd dreamed of building.

Then, there was nothing at all.

SEVEN
THE HIDDEN LIBRARY

Lyra's boots echoed on ancient stone as she descended the winding staircase. Cobwebs clung to her hair, and the musty scent of forgotten tomes filled her nostrils. Beside her, Darius held a glowing orb of magic, casting eerie shadows on the walls.

"How much further?" Lyra whispered, her voice seeming too loud in the silence.

Darius shook his head. "I'm not sure. The ancient texts were... vague about the exact location of the library."

Lyra bit back a sigh of frustration. They had searched for days, following cryptic clues and half-remembered legends. All the while, the rebel camp grew more restless, more divided.

The stairs ended abruptly, opening into a vast chamber. Lyra's breath caught in her throat. Row upon row of towering bookshelves stretched before them, disappearing into the darkness.

"By the old gods," Darius breathed. "It's real."

Lyra stepped forward, running her fingers along leather-bound spines. Titles in languages she'd never seen glimmered in the magical light. "Where do we even begin?"

Darius moved to a nearby pedestal where an enormous tome lay open. "Here, I think. This looks like some sort of index."

As he pored over the ancient text, Lyra wandered deeper into the library. The weight of history pressed down on her, along with the responsibility of her bloodline. Somewhere in this labyrinth of knowledge lay the answers she sought. The key to controlling her growing powers, to fulfilling the prophecy, to saving Aethoria.

"Lyra!" Darius' excited voice broke through her thoughts. "I think I found something!"

She rushed back to his side. He pointed to a passage in the index, his eyes bright with discovery.

"'The Convergence of Royal and Elemental Magic,'" he read aloud. "'A treatise on the unique powers of the Valenwood line.' This must be what we're looking for."

Lyra's heart raced. "Where is it?"

Darius squinted at the text. "Section 17, shelf 394. Whatever that means."

They set off into the maze of bookshelves, Darius' magical light bobbing before them. As they walked, Lyra found her gaze drawn to it. In the soft glow, the sharp angles of his face seemed softer, more vulnerable.

"Why are you helping me?" The question slipped out before she could stop herself.

Darius looked at her, surprise flickering across his features. "What do you mean?"

Lyra pressed on, needing to understand. "You gave up every-thing. Your position in the Vanguard, your life in Solara. Why?"

He was silent for a long moment, his brow furrowed in thought. When he spoke, his voice was deep and intense. "Because it's right. Because what the Vanguard is doing... it's not what I signed up for. And because-" He trailed off, looking away.

"Because what?" Lyra nudged gently.

Darius met her gaze, and the raw emotion there took her breath away. "Because of you," he said simply. "From the moment we met in that clearing, I knew... I knew my life would never be the same again."

Lyra's heart thundered in her chest. She opened her mouth to reply, but a gleam of gold caught her eye. "Look," she said instead, pointing. "Section 17."

They turned down the aisle, scanning the shelves. Lyra's fingers tingled with anticipation as they approached shelf 394.

"There!" Darius exclaimed, reaching for a thick, ornate volume.

The moment his fingers brushed the spine, a surge of energy pulsed through the air. Lyra stumbled back as the bookcase swung outward, revealing a hidden chamber beyond.

"Are you all right?" Darius steadied her with a hand on her arm.

Lyra nodded, too stunned to speak. Together they entered the secret room.

It was smaller than the main library, but every surface was covered in intricate runes and diagrams. In the center stood a pedestal upon which rested a single book bound in midnight blue leather.

Lyra approached it slowly, drawn by an inexplicable pull. As her fingers touched the cover, the gem in her crown pulsed with answering light.

"This is it," she whispered. "The answers we've been seeking."

With trembling hands, she opened the book. Pages of elegant writing and detailed illustrations greeted her. She began to read aloud:

"To those of Valenwood blood who seek to understand their gift and burden, hear these words. The magic that flows through your veins is not merely power, but a sacred trust. It is the lifeblood of Aethoria itself, a link to the very heart of our land.'"

Darius leaned forward, his shoulder brushing hers. "'But beware,'" he continued reading, "'for with great power comes great danger. The union of royal and elemental magic creates a power beyond measure. One that, if left unchecked, could tear at the very fabric of our world.'"

Lyra's blood ran cold. "Is this what is happening to me? Am I... am I a danger to everyone around me?"

Darius' hand found hers and squeezed gently. "Keep reading," he urged. "There must be more."

Lyra took a deep breath and turned the page. Her eyes widened when she saw a familiar picture. "Darius, look. It's the Crown of Whispers."

The illustration showed the delicate diadem she now wore, surrounded by swirling patterns of energy.

"'The Crown of Whispers,'" Lyra read, "'forged in the dawn of our kingdom, serves as both catalyst and conduit. It amplifies the wearer's power while providing a measure of control. But true mastery comes not from the crown, but from within."'

She looked up at Darius, hope blossoming in her chest. "There is a way to control it. To use that power without destroying everything."

Darius nodded, his eyes bright with excitement. "And look here," he pointed to another passage. "'The full potential of Valenwood magic can only be realized through balance. The union of opposing forces, the harmony of chaos and order.'"

Lyra frowned. "What does that mean? How do I find that balance?"

Before Darius could answer, a distant boom echoed through the library. Dust rained down from the ceiling as the ground shook beneath their feet.

"What was that?" Lyra gasped, steadying herself against the pedestal.

Darius' face hardened. "Trouble. We have to go. Now."

Lyra hesitated, glancing back at the book. "But we've barely scratched the surface. There's still so much to learn."

Another crack, closer this time. The shelves around them shook ominously.

Darius grabbed her shoulders, his eyes intense. "Lyra, listen to me. This book is important, yes. But you are the key. Everything we need is already inside you. We have to get you to safety."

She wanted to argue, to insist on staying until they'd uncovered every secret. But the urgency in Darius's voice, the genuine fear in his eyes, made her pause.

"All right," she said finally. "But we're taking the book."

Darius nodded, already heading for the exit. "Grab it and let's go."

Lyra grabbed the tome from its pedestal and clutched it to her chest. As they ran back through the main chamber, the sounds of destruction grew louder.

"How did they find us?" Lyra panted as they reached the stairs.

Darius' jaw clenched. "I don't know. But I intend to find out."

They burst out of the hidden entrance and into the pre-dawn forest. The rebel camp was in chaos. Tents were burning, people were running in all directions, and the clash of steel on steel filled the air.

"Vanguard!" Someone shouted. "They're everywhere!"

Lyra's heart sank as she took in the scene. How could everything have gone so wrong so quickly?

A figure broke away from the melee and ran toward them. Aren, his face streaked with blood and soot.

"Where have you been?" He yelled as he reached them. "We're under attack!"

"We can see that," Darius snapped. "How did this happen?"

Aren's eyes narrowed in suspicion. "Funny you should ask. They seemed to know exactly where to find us. Almost like someone told them."

The accusation hung in the air between them. Lyra opened her mouth to defend Darius, but a scream cut her off.

Mira stumbled into view, a Vanguard soldier hot on her heels. Without thinking, Lyra reached out. Raw power surged through her, stronger than ever. A bolt of blue energy struck the soldier, sending him flying backward.

Mira collapsed into Lyra's arms, sobbing. "They came out of nowhere," she choked out. "So many of them."

Lyra looked from Mira to Aren to Darius, her mind racing. They needed a plan, they needed to regroup and-

A blast of horn cut through the chaos. Lyra's blood ran cold as she recognized the signal.

"Archmage Calidus," Darius whispered, his face pale. "He's here."

Lyra clutched the book tighter, her other hand going to the Crown of Whispers. Everything they'd just learned, everything they'd fought for, hung in the balance.

"What do we do?" Aren demanded, looking to her for guidance.

Lyra took a deep breath and squared her shoulders. The answer came to her with startling clarity.

"We fight," she said, her voice full of determination. "We fight, and we win. Because we have to."

As if in response to her words, the gem in her crown pulsed with brilliant light. Lyra felt the magic surge within her, no longer a chaotic force, but a focused stream of power.

She met Darius's gaze and saw her own determination reflected in it. Whatever came next, they would face it together.

The battle for the future of Aethoria had truly begun.

EIGHT
FORBIDDEN FEELINGS

Moonlight filtered through the canopy of the Whispering Grove, casting mottled shadows on the forest floor. Lyra stood at the edge of the rebel camp, her eyes closed, focusing on the throbbing energy within her. The Crown of Whispers pulsed gently on her forehead, a constant reminder of her destiny.

"Your Majesty?" Darius' voice broke her concentration.

Lyra's eyes snapped open. "Don't call me that," she said, sharper than she intended.

Darius raised an eyebrow. "Would you prefer 'my lady'? Or 'O great and powerful one'?"

Despite herself, Lyra felt a smile tug at her lips. "How about 'Lyra'? You know, my real name?"

"As you wish... Lyra." The way he said her name sent a shiver down her spine.

She turned to face him fully, taking in the way the moonlight caught his features. "Did you need something?"

Darius nodded, his expression growing serious. "The war council is meeting. Aren says they have a plan for a major strike against the Vanguard."

Lyra's heart quickened. This might be the opportunity they'd been waiting for. "Lead the way," she said.

As they walked through the camp, Lyra was aware of Darius' presence beside her. The back of his hand brushed against hers, sending sparks of electricity through her body. She clenched her fist and tried to concentrate on the task at hand.

They entered the large tent that served as their command center. Maps and charts covered every surface, and the air buzzed with excitement. Aren looked up as they entered, his eyes narrowing slightly at their proximity.

"Nice of you to join us," he said, his tone clipped.

Lyra chose to ignore the barb. "What's the situation?"

Thorne, hunched over a map, straightened with a groan. "We've received information about a Vanguard supply convoy heading for the southern coast. If we can intercept it, we'll deal a significant blow to their operations."

"And gain much needed resources for our cause," Mira added, her young face aglow with excitement.

Lyra studied the map, tracing the planned route of the convoy with her finger. "It's risky. We'll be exposed on the open road."

"That's why we strike here," Aren said, pointing to a narrow pass between two hills. "We can funnel them into a choke point, negating their numerical advantage."

Darius leaned forward, his shoulder brushing Lyra's. She inhaled sharply at the contact, catching a whiff of pine and something unique... him.

"The terrain favors an ambush," Darius mused, seemingly unaware of Lyra's reaction. "But they'll be expecting it. The Vanguard leaves nothing to chance."

Aren's jaw clenched. "And how do you know that?"

The tension in the tent rose a notch. Lyra stepped in before things could escalate. "Because he was one of them, Aren. Which makes his insight invaluable."

She turned to Darius. "What do you suggest?"

He met her gaze, and for a moment the rest of the world fell away. Then he blinked and refocused on the map. "A two-pronged attack. One group here, at the choke point, to get their attention. Meanwhile, a smaller force strikes from behind, targeting the supply wagons directly."

Lyra nodded slowly, the plan taking shape in her mind. "It could work. But it's dangerous. Whoever leads the second group will be taking a huge risk."

"I'll do it," Darius said without hesitation.

"No." The word escaped Lyra's lips before she could stop it. All eyes turned to her, and she struggled to recover. "I mean... we can't risk our best tactical minds on such a dangerous mission."

Aren's eyes narrowed. "Funny. I thought our 'best tactical mind' was right here." He tapped his own temple.

The tap hung in the air, heavy with implication. Lyra opened her mouth to reply, but Thorne cut her off.

"Enough," the old man said, his voice carrying the weight of years of command. "We can argue about who's smarter later. Right now we need to finish this plan."

For the next hour, they worked out the details of the attack.

As the others filed out of the tent, Lyra found herself lingering, not quite ready to leave Darius' presence.

He must have sensed her hesitation, for he turned back, concern etched into his features. "Lyra? Is everything all right?"

She nodded, not trusting her voice. He took a step closer, close enough that she could feel the heat radiating from his body.

"You've been... different lately," he said quietly. "Distracted. If there's anything I can do to help-"

"There isn't," Lyra cut him off, harsher than she intended. She saw the hurt flash across his face and immediately regretted her words. "I'm sorry, I... I have a lot on my mind."

Darius' expression softened. "I can imagine. The weight of a kingdom on your shoulders, a rebel army looking to you for leadership, and a power you're only beginning to understand."

Lyra let out a shaky breath. "When you put it like that, it sounds impossible."

"It's not impossible," Darius said, his voice deep and intense. "You're the strongest person I've ever known, Lyra. You can do this. And you won't have to do it alone."

Before she could stop herself, Lyra reached out and placed her hand on his chest. She could feel his heart racing beneath her palm, matching the frantic beat of her own.

"Darius, I-"

The tent flap rustled and they jumped apart as Aren entered. He froze, taking in the scene before him, his eyes darkening with suspicion.

"Am I interrupting something?" he asked, his voice dangerously calm.

Lyra straightened, forcing her voice to remain calm. "Not at all. We were discussing the strategy for the ambush."

Aren's eyes darted between them, clearly not believing her. "I see. Well, if you're done 'discussing strategy,' we need to begin preparations. The convoy leaves at dawn."

With a final, pointed look, he ducked out of the tent. Lyra let out a breath she hadn't realized she was holding.

"We should go," she said, not meeting Darius' eyes.

He nodded, his expression unreadable. "Of course. Your Majesty."

The formality stung more than she had expected. As Darius turned to leave, Lyra's hand shot out and grabbed his wrist. He turned, surprise and hope warring on his face.

For a moment they stood frozen, the air between them crackling with unspoken desire. Then, as if drawn by an unseen force, they moved toward each other.

Their lips met in a kiss that was both tender and desperate. Lyra's hands tangled in Darius' hair as his arms wrapped around her waist, pulling her closer. The world fell away, leaving only the sensation of his lips on hers, the warmth of his body pressed against hers.

When they finally broke apart, both gasping for air, reality came crashing back. Lyra stepped back, her fingers going to her lips.

"We can't," she whispered, her voice breaking. "This... us... it's impossible."

Darius reached for her, but she shook her head and pulled away. "Lyra, please..."

"No," she said, more firmly this time. "I'm sorry, Darius. But I have a duty to my people. I can't let my personal feelings get in the way of that."

With that, she turned and fled the tent, leaving Darius standing alone in the flickering lamplight.

Outside, the cool night air did little to calm the storm raging inside her. Lyra's mind reeled, torn between the lingering warmth of Darius' kiss and the cold reality of her responsibilities.

As she made her way back to her own tent, a figure emerged from the shadows. Aren.

"Enjoying your evening stroll?" he asked, his voice dripping with sarcasm.

Lyra straightened and squared her shoulders. "What I do with my time is not your concern, Aren."

He stepped closer, his eyes blazing with a mixture of anger and concern. "It is when it affects the safety of everyone in this camp. Do you have any idea how dangerous that is?"

"Nothing happened," Lyra lied, the taste of Darius still on her lips.

Aren's laugh was bitter. "Right. And I suppose you were 'discussing strategy' with your tongues?"

Lyra flinched as if hit. "You were spying on us?"

"I was protecting you," Aren shot back. "He's Vanguard, Lyra. Or have you forgotten? How do you know this isn't all part of some elaborate plan to infiltrate our ranks?"

"He's proven himself," Lyra said, but doubt crept into her voice.

Aren shook his head. "Has he? Or has he proven himself to be an excellent actor?" He put a hand on her shoulder, his voice softening. "I care about you, Lyra. We all do. But this... whatever it is between you and Darius... it threatens everything we've fought for."

With that, he turned and walked away, leaving Lyra alone with her thoughts.

She looked up at the stars, sparkling coldly in the vast expanse of the sky. Tomorrow they would strike against the Vanguard, risking everything for a daring plan. And Lyra would have to lead them, putting aside her conflicted heart for the good of her people.

As she crawled into her tent, exhaustion finally overtaking her, a thought echoed through her mind:

What have I done?

The answer, she realized, could change everything.

NINE
TRUST DIVIDED

Dawn broke over the hills, painting the sky with shades of pink and gold. Lyra crouched behind a rock, her eyes fixed on the road below. The air crackled with tension as the rebels waited for the Vanguard convoy to arrive.

"Any sign?" Aren whispered, his breath misting in the cool morning air.

Lyra shook her head. "Nothing yet."

Her mind wandered to Darius, leading the second group on the other side of the pass. The memory of their kiss burned in her mind, a distraction she couldn't afford. She pushed it aside and focused on the task at hand.

A low whistle broke the silence - the signal. Lyra's heart raced as she looked around the rocks. The convoy emerged from the fog, a line of wagons heavily guarded by Vanguard soldiers.

"Remember the plan," Lyra murmured to the rebels around her. "Wait for my signal."

The convoy drew closer, the creaking of wagon wheels and the clanking of armor growing louder. Lyra's fingers tingled with magic, ready to be unleashed. She raised her hand, ready to give the order-

"Ambush!" A Vanguard soldier's cry shattered the morning calm.

Chaos erupted. Vanguard mages threw up shields as arrows rained down from the hillsides. How had they known?

"It's a trap!" Aren roared. "Fall back!"

Lyra's mind raced. This was all wrong. They should have had the element of surprise. Unless...

No time to think. She leapt from cover, magic coursing through her veins. A wave of energy burst from her hands, slamming into the vanguard's front line. Soldiers stumbled, their formation broken.

"Push through!" Lyra yelled to her rebels. "Get to those wagons!"

The rebels charged down the hill, clashing with the vanguard in a frenzy of steel and magic. Lyra weaved through the melee, parrying attacks and striking where she could. But for every soldier she felled, two more seemed to take their place.

A familiar voice cut through the din. "Lyra! Behind you!"

She spun to see Darius emerge from the trees, his face streaked with dirt and blood. Relief washed over her, quickly replaced by confusion. Why wasn't he with the second group?

Before she could ask, a bolt of energy sizzled past her ear. She turned to see a Vanguard mage preparing for another attack. Lyra raised her hands, ready to counter.

The mage's eyes widened in surprise as a sword erupted from his chest. He crumpled to reveal Aren, his blade dripping red.

"We have to retreat," Aren panted. "There are too many of them."

Lyra nodded grimly. "Sound the horn. Get our people out of here."

As the mournful blast echoed through the valley, Lyra caught Darius' eye. The look that passed between them spoke volumes. Relief, fear, and something deeper that neither dared to name.

The rebels melted back into the forest, the sounds of pursuit fading behind them. Lyra's mind raced as they ran. How had the Vanguard known of their plan? The implications chilled her to the bone.

Hours later, Lyra stood in the command tent, her shoulders slumped with exhaustion. The failed ambush had cost her dearly - in lives, resources, and morale.

"How did this happen?" Thorne's weathered voice broke the heavy silence. "We planned for every contingency."

"Not every contingency," Aren said, his eyes hard as he looked at Darius. "Would you like to explain why you weren't with your group when the attack began?"

Darius stiffened. "We were ambushed before we could get into position. I came to warn you, but it was too late."

"Convenient," Aren spat. "The Vanguard is suddenly three steps ahead of us, and you're always in the right place at the wrong time."

"What are you implying?" Darius took a step forward, magic crackling at his fingertips.

Aren's hand went to his sword. "I think you know exactly what I'm implying, Vanguard."

"Enough!" Lyra's voice cracked like a whip. "This infighting solves nothing. We need to find out how the Vanguard anticipated our moves."

"I'll tell you how," Aren said, his voice deep and dangerous. "We have a traitor in our midst."

The accusation hung in the air, heavy as a storm cloud. Lyra's eyes darted between Aren and Darius, seeing the suspicion, the anger, the fear.

"You can't seriously think..." Darius began.

Aren cut him off. "Can't I? You show up out of nowhere, claiming to want to help. You gain our trust, learn our secrets. And suddenly the Vanguard is always one step ahead."

"If I wanted to betray you, I've had a hundred chances," Darius shot back. "I risked my life for this, for Lyra-"

"Oh yes, for Lyra," Aren's voice dripped with sarcasm. "We've all seen how close you two have become."

Lyra's cheeks burned. "That's enough, Aren."

But he continued, turning to face her. "Is it? Because from where I'm standing, it looks like you're letting your emotions cloud your judgment. Putting everyone in danger because you can't see what's right in front of you."

"And what's that?" Lyra asked, her voice dangerously calm.

Aren's eyes bored into hers. "That he's using you. Using all of us. And you're too blinded by... whatever this is between you to see it."

The words hit Lyra like a physical blow. She opened her mouth to respond, but no sound came out.

Darius stepped forward, his face a mask of barely contained

rage. "You don't know what you're talking about. I would never betray Lyra. Or any of you."

"Prove it," Aren challenged. "Prove that you're not feeding information to the Vanguard."

"How?" Darius spread his arms wide. "How can I prove a negative?"

The tension in the tent was unbearable. Lyra looked from Aren to Darius, seeing the pain and anger in their faces. These were the two people she trusted most in the world, and now...

"Lyra," Thorne's soft voice cut through her thoughts. "What do you think?"

All eyes turned to her. The weight of command, of expectation, pressed on her shoulders. She took a deep breath, forcing her voice to remain calm.

"I think... we need to consider all possibilities. Including the possibility that there is a traitor among us."

Darius recoiled as if hit. "You can't be serious."

"I'm not accusing you," Lyra said quickly. "But Aren's right. The Vanguard has been anticipating our every move. We need to find out why."

"And how do you suggest we do that?" Thorne asked.

Lyra squared her shoulders. "We feed them false information. Set a trap of our own."

Aren nodded slowly. "It could work. But we'd have to keep it quiet. Only a select few can know the real plan."

"Agreed," Lyra said. "Thorne, I want you to spread the word of a major attack on the Vanguard's southern outpost. Make it convincing."

The old man nodded, understanding dawning in his eyes.

"Meanwhile," Lyra continued, "we will make our real move elsewhere. Something small, surgical. A team of our best fighters to strike where they least expect it."

"And who will lead this team?" Aren asked, his eyes narrowing.

Lyra met his gaze unflinchingly. "I do."

A chorus of protests erupted, but Lyra raised her hand for silence. "This is not up for debate. I need to see for myself what we're up against."

She turned to Darius, her heart aching at the pain in his eyes. "I'm sorry, but you have to stay behind. We can't risk..."

"Can't risk what?" Darius cut her off, his voice bitter. "Can't risk me betraying you? Or can't risk your feelings getting in the way?"

Lyra winced. "That's not fair."

"Isn't it?" Darius shook his head. "You say you trust me, but your actions tell a different story."

Without another word, he stormed out of the tent. Lyra started to follow, but Aren's hand on her arm stopped her.

"Let him go," he said quietly. "We have work to do."

Lyra nodded, pushing down the pain in her chest. She turned back to the others, forcing herself to focus on the task at hand.

"All right," she said, her voice stronger than she felt. "Here's the plan..."

As they huddled over maps and discussed strategy, Lyra couldn't shake the feeling that everything was falling apart. The trust that held their rebellion together was fracturing, and she didn't know how to mend it.

And somewhere out there, the Vanguard waited. Watching. Ready to strike again.

The real question was: would the rebels tear themselves apart before the Vanguard had a chance?

Only time would tell. And time, Lyra feared, was running out.

TEN

THE PRICE OF MAGIC

Lyra stood at the edge of a clearing in the Whispering Grove, her eyes closed, concentrating on the energy pulsing through her veins. The Crown of Whispers hummed on her forehead, its power intertwined with her own.

"Focus," Darius' voice came from behind her. "Feel the magic of the land. Let it flow through you."

Lyra gritted her teeth. "I'm trying."

"Don't try. Do."

She opened one eye to look at him. "You're enjoying this, aren't you?"

The ghost of a smile played on Darius' lips. "Maybe a little. Now concentrate."

Lyra closed her eyes again, reaching out with her senses. The forest hummed with life - the whisper of leaves, the pulse of sap in ancient trees, the scurrying of small creatures in the underbrush. She let it wash over her, feeling the ebb and flow of natural magic.

"Good," Darius murmured. "Now channel it. Bend it to your will."

Lyra held out her hand, imagining the magic coalescing into a ball of pure energy. She felt it gather, build -

A crack like thunder split the air. Lyra's eyes flew open as a shockwave erupted from her palm, sending her stumbling backward. Trees groaned and swayed, leaves whirling in a sudden windstorm.

"Lyra!" Darius caught her before she fell, his arms strong and firm around her waist.

For a moment, they stood frozen, their faces inches apart. Lyra's heart raced, and she wasn't sure if it was from the magical reaction or Darius' closeness.

She pulled away first, straightening her tunic. "Well, that didn't go as planned."

Darius ran a hand through his hair, looking worried. "Your power is growing faster than I expected. We need to find a way for you to control it before..."

"Before what?" Lyra challenged. "Before I level half the forest? Before I hurt someone?"

"Before the Vanguard realizes the full extent of what you can do," Darius finished quietly.

Lyra's shoulders sagged. "And how am I supposed to control something I barely understand?"

Darius stepped closer, his expression softening. "The same way you've handled everything else - one step at a time." He held out his hand. "Come on. I want to show you something."

Curiosity overcame her frustration. Lyra took his hand, ignoring the spark that shot through her at the contact. Darius led her deeper into the forest, ducking under low-hanging branches and around moss-covered boulders.

They emerged into another clearing, this one dominated by a massive oak. Its trunk was wider than Lyra could wrap her arms around, its branches reaching skyward like gnarled fingers.

"What is this place?" Lyra breathed, feeling the power emanating from the ancient tree.

"A nexus," Darius explained. "A point where the natural magic of the land comes together. The Vanguard has forgotten about places like this, but they are the key to understanding your power."

He led them to the base of the tree. "Place your hand on the trunk. Listen to what it tells you."

Lyra raised an eyebrow. "The tree will talk to me?"

"In a manner of speaking," Darius said with a hint of a smile. "Trust me."

Lyra pressed the palm of her hand against the rough bark. At first, she felt nothing but the texture of the wood against her skin. Then, slowly, a warmth began to spread up her arm. Images flashed through her mind - seasons changing in an instant, roots spreading deep into the earth, branches reaching for the sunlight.

She gasped and pulled her hand away. "I saw... everything. The entire history of this place."

Darius nodded. "This is the magic of Aethoria itself. It's what you're connected to, what gives you your power. The Vanguard tries to control it, to bend it to their will. But you..." He trailed off, his eyes intense. "You're part of it."

Lyra's mind reeled at the implications. "So how do I control it?"

"You don't," Darius said simply. "You work with it. Guide it, not force it."

He stepped behind her, close enough that she could feel the warmth of his body. "Try again. This time, don't force the magic. Let it flow through you, like water through a canal."

Lyra took a deep breath and put her hand back on the trunk. She closed her eyes and concentrated on the feeling of the magic flowing through her. Instead of trying to shape it into any particular form, she imagined herself as a conduit, directing the flow.

The air around her began to shimmer. Leaves rustled without wind, and the grass at her feet seemed to grow and sway on its own. Lyra opened her eyes to see tendrils of blue energy weaving between her fingers, dancing in intricate patterns.

"I do," she whispered, awe in her voice.

Darius' hand came to rest on her shoulder. "You are. This is just the beginning, Lyra. With practice, you'll be able to..."

A scream cut through the air, shattering the moment. The magic dissipated as Lyra spun toward the sound.

"It came from the camp," Darius said, already moving.

They raced through the forest, branches whipping at their faces. As they neared the rebel encampment, the shouts and clash of steel grew louder.

They burst into the camp to find it in chaos. Rebels struggled with shadowy figures, their forms flickering and distorting in impossible ways.

"What are those things?" Lyra gasped.

Darius' face paled. "Shadow constructs. Calidus' work. But how did they find us?"

There was no time to ponder the question. A construct lunged at them, its claws ripping the air where Lyra's head had been a moment before. She ducked, rolled to the side, and came up with her hands raised.

Magic surged through her, different than before - raw, instinctive. A bolt of energy shot from her palms, hitting the construct square in the chest. It dissipated with an eerie shriek.

Around them, the rebels fought valiantly, but they were outnumbered. The constructs seemed to shrug off normal weapons, reforming even as blades passed through them.

"Lyra!" Aren's voice cut through the noise. She turned to see him fighting two constructs, his sword passing harmlessly through their smoky forms.

Without thinking, Lyra thrust out her hands. The magic responded instantly, surging forth in a wave of pure power. The constructs were blasted backward, disintegrating into shadows.

Aren stared at her, a mixture of awe and fear on his face. "How did you..."

"No time," Lyra cut him off. "We have to evacuate the camp. These things will keep coming."

Aren nodded, already shouting orders to the other rebels. Lyra turned and searched the chaos for Darius. She spotted him across the clearing, his hands weaving complex patterns as he held off three constructs at once.

Lyra started toward him, but a scream stopped her. Mira lay on the ground, a construct looming over her, its claws ready to strike.

Time seemed to slow. Lyra saw Mira's terrified face, saw the construct's arm begin to fall. She reached out with her magic, desperate to stop it-

Power exploded from her in a blinding flash of blue light. The air itself seemed to ripple, and for a moment all was silent.

When Lyra's vision cleared, she gasped. The construct that had attacked Mira was gone, along with every other shadow creature in sight. But so were the tents closest to her, reduced to tattered shreds. Trees at the edge of the camp had been uprooted, and a deep furrow had been cut in the ground.

Rebels picked themselves up from the ground and stared at Lyra with a mixture of awe and fear. She looked down at her hands, still crackling with residual energy.

"Lyra?" Darius' voice was tentative as he approached. "Are you all right?"

She met his gaze, seeing the concern there. "I... I don't know. What did I do?"

Before he could answer, Aren's voice rang out. "Everyone, gather what you can carry. We have to move, now. It's not safe here anymore."

As the camp erupted into frantic activity, Lyra stood rooted to the spot. The full weight of what had happened crashed down on her. She'd saved them, yes, but at what cost? The destruction around her was a stark reminder of the power she wielded - power she still couldn't fully control.

Darius' hand on her arm brought her back to reality. "We should go," he said quietly.

Lyra nodded, forcing herself to move. But as they joined the stream of rebels fleeing into the forest, a thought echoed in her mind:

If this was the price of magic, was she willing - or able - to pay it?

The answer, she feared, might determine the fate of Aethoria itself.

ELEVEN
SHADOWS OF DOUBT

Lyra's boots sank into the mud as she trudged through the forest, leading the ragged band of rebels. Three days of constant movement had taken their toll. Exhaustion etched deep lines on every face, and supplies dwindled with each passing hour.

"We have to stop," Aren said, falling into step beside her. "The people can't go on like this."

Lyra shook her head. "We can't risk it. The Vanguard could be right behind us."

"And if we keep going, we'll collapse before they even find us," Aren argued. His voice softened. "Lyra, they need rest. We all do."

She looked back at the group. Children clung to their parents' hands, older villagers leaned heavily on makeshift walking sticks. Even the hardened rebels showed signs of wear.

"Fine," Lyra conceded. "We'll stop at the next clearing. But just for a few hours."

Aren nodded, relief written all over his face. As he moved to spread the word, Lyra caught snippets of muffled conversation.

"...can't keep running forever..."

"...never should have left the old camp..."

"...their fault we're in this mess..."

The words stung, but Lyra forced herself to keep moving. She couldn't let them see her doubt, her fear. She was their leader, whether she liked it or not.

A flash of movement caught her eye. Darius materialized from the shadows, his face grim.

"Any sign of pursuit?" Lyra asked.

He shook his head. "Nothing. It's too quiet."

"You say that like it's a bad thing."

"It could be," Darius said, his brow furrowed. "The Vanguard doesn't give up that easily. They're planning something."

Before Lyra could respond, a cry rang out from the rear of the group. They turned to see a young rebel pointing to the sky.

"Look!"

A black figure soared above them, its wings blocking out the sun for a moment. Lyra's blood ran cold. A Vanguard Scout Drake.

"Everyone, take cover!" she yelled.

The group scattered, diving for any cover they could find. Lyra pressed herself against a tree trunk, her heart pounding. The drake circled once, twice, then disappeared behind the tree line.

For a long moment, no one moved. Then, slowly, people began to come out of hiding.

"Did it see us?" Mira asked, her voice shaking.

"I don't know," Lyra admitted. She turned to Darius. "If it did, how long do we have?"

His expression was grim. "An hour. Maybe less."

Panic swept through the group. Voices rose, overlapping in a cacophony of fear and anger.

"We can't keep running!"

"This is hopeless!"

"We should never have followed her!"

The last comment cut deepest. Lyra felt the weight of their looks, their doubts, their accusations.

"Enough!" Aren's voice rose above the din. "This solves nothing. We need a plan."

All eyes turned to Lyra. She squared her shoulders and forced confidence into her voice. "Aren's right. We can't outrun them, so we fight. We find a defensible position and make our stand."

Murmurs of disagreement rippled through the crowd. An older man - Finnian, the herbalist from Oakridge - stepped forward.

"With all due respect, Your Majesty," he said, the title carrying a hint of sarcasm, "we are not soldiers. We're farmers, craftsmen. How can we hope to stand against the Vanguard?"

"We have no choice," Lyra countered. "If we keep running, we'll die exhausted and alone. At least this way we have a chance."

"A chance at what?" someone in the crowd shouted. "Getting slaughtered?"

The situation was getting out of hand. Lyra could feel her tenuous grip on leadership slipping away. She opened her mouth to reply, but Darius beat her to it.

"You're right," he said, his voice carrying across the clearing. "You are not soldiers. But neither were the people who first stood against the tyranny of the Vanguard. Nor was Lyra when she took up this cause."

He moved to stand beside her, his presence a steadying force. "I have seen what the Vanguard can do. I've been a part of it. And I can tell you, they are not invincible. They are not gods. They are men and women, fallible and afraid."

Darius' eyes swept the crowd. "You have something they don't. Something they can never understand. You have a cause worth fighting for. A future worth believing in."

The words hung in the air, their effect visible on the faces of the rebels and the villagers. Lyra felt a surge of gratitude, tinged with a hint of something deeper.

"He's right," she said, finding her voice again. "We may not be an army, but we have something more powerful. We have each other. And we have hope."

She pointed to a rock in the distance. "There. We make our stand there. Those who can fight will fight. Those who can't will support in other ways. But we do it together."

A moment of silence stretched out, tight as a bowstring. Then, slowly, nods of agreement rippled through the crowd. The spark of determination rekindled in their eyes.

As the group began to move toward the ledge, Aren approached Lyra and Darius.

"That was well done," he said reluctantly. "Both of you."

Lyra nodded, grateful for the little olive branch. "We're not out of danger yet. We need to prepare."

"I'll organize defensive positions," Aren said. "See what weapons we can cobble together."

As he left, Lyra turned to Darius. "Thank you," she said quietly. "For what you said before."

He met her gaze, his eyes intense. "I meant every word."

For a moment, the rest of the world fell away. Lyra found herself drawn to him, the memory of their kiss burning in her mind.

A commotion from the group brought her back to reality. She stepped back and cleared her throat. "We should... we should help with the preparations."

Darius nodded, a flicker of disappointment crossing his face. "Of course."

As they moved to join the others, Lyra couldn't shake the feeling that everything was about to change. For better or worse, the next few hours would determine the fate of her rebellion.

The sun sank lower on the horizon as the rebels fortified their position. Crude barricades rose from gathered rocks and fallen trees. Those with battle experience drilled the others in basic defensive maneuvers. The air buzzed with nervous energy.

Lyra stood at the highest point of the promontory and surveyed their makeshift fortress. It wasn't much, but it was all they had.

"Your Majesty?"

She turned to see Thorne approaching, his weathered face grave. "What is it?"

The old man hesitated. "There's... something you need to see."

Fear clenched in Lyra's stomach as she followed Thorne to a small tent they'd set up as a command post. Inside, Aren and Darius stood over a makeshift table, their faces grim.

"What's going on?" Lyra demanded.

Aren held up a small crystal - a Vanguard communication device. "We found this hidden among our supplies."

The implications hit Lyra like a physical blow. "A spy? Here? But how..."

"It gets worse," Darius interrupted. He gestured to a map spread out on the table. "Based on the last transmission, the Vanguard knows exactly where we are. And they're coming in force."

Lyra's mind raced. A spy in their midst. The Vanguard bearing down on them. And a group of exhausted, ill-equipped rebels as their only defense.

"How long do we have?" she asked, her voice calmer than she felt.

"An hour," Darius replied. "Two at the most."

Aren's hand went to the hilt of his sword. "We must root out the traitor. Now."

"And start a witch hunt?" Thorne shook his head. "That's what the Vanguard wants. We'd be tearing ourselves apart before they even get here."

"So we do nothing?" Aren challenged.

"No," Lyra said, her voice cutting through the argument. "We prepare. We fight. And we show the Vanguard-and whoever this traitor is-that we will not be broken."

She met each of their eyes in turn. "Spread the word. Every able-bodied person to the walls. Children, the elderly, and the wounded in the center, protected. And I want guards on our supplies. No one touches them without permission."

As the others moved to carry out her orders, Darius lingered. "Lyra," he said quietly. "There's something else you need to know."

She braced herself. "What is it?"

"The Vanguard force..." He hesitated. "Archmage Calidus leads them personally."

The news hit Lyra like a punch to the gut. Calidus. The most powerful mage in Aethoria, and the architect of the Vanguard's tyranny.

"Well," she said, forcing a wry smile, "I suppose we should be flattered. He thinks we're important enough to be dealt with personally."

Darius didn't return the smile. "Lyra, this is serious. If Calidus comes..."

"I know," she cut him off. "But we can't change that now. We can only face what is coming."

He nodded slowly. "Together?"

Lyra met his gaze, saw the determination there, the unwavering support. Despite everything, she felt a flicker of hope.

"Together," she agreed.

As they stepped out of the tent, a blast of horn split the air. Aren's voice rang out across the camp.

"Vanguard sighted! All to positions!"

Lyra's hand went to the Crown of Whispers, feeling its power pulse in time with her racing heart. This was it. The moment that would decide everything.

She looked out over the rebels - her people - as they scrambled to their posts. Peasants clutching makeshift spears. Children wide-eyed with fear. And in every face, a glimmer of hope, of determination.

Lyra raised her voice, letting it carry over the ledge. "Stand firm! Whatever comes, we will face it as one! For Aethoria!"

The cry was taken up, echoing into the gathering darkness. "For Aethoria!"

As the first Vanguard banners appeared on the horizon, Lyra steeled herself for the battle ahead. Win or lose, the fate of the kingdom would be decided here.

And she would be ready.

TWELVE
HEART'S DIVIDE

The air crackled with tension as Lyra stood atop the makeshift fortress, her eyes fixed on the horizon. The vanguard forces were advancing like a tide of steel and magic, their numbers seeming to grow with each passing moment.

"They'll be in range soon," Aren said, his voice tense with barely contained fear. "What are your orders?"

Lyra's mind raced, weighing her limited options. "Have our archers ready. We can't match their numbers, but we can make them pay for every inch they gain."

Aren nodded and moved to relay the order. As he left, Darius took his place at Lyra's side.

"You should be with the other mages," Lyra said, not taking her eyes off the approaching army. "We're going to need every ounce of magical power we can muster."

"My place is here," Darius replied, his tone brooking no argument. "Besides, someone needs to stop you from doing something stupidly heroic."

Despite the dire circumstances, Lyra felt a smile tug at her lips. "Me? Never."

Her moment of levity was shattered by a thunderous boom. The air shimmered as a massive magical barrier sprang into existence, encircling the rebel stronghold.

"What the..." Lyra's exclamation was cut short as a figure materialized before them in a swirl of arcane energy.

Archmage Calidus stood only a few feet away, his ornate robes billowing in a wind that seemed to touch no one else. His eyes, cold and calculating, were fixed on Lyra.

"So," he said, his voice carrying easily despite the chaos around them. "The lost princess finally reveals herself."

Lyra's hand went to the Crown of Whispers, its power humming in response to her surging emotions. "I am not lost, Calidus. I'm right where I need to be."

The Archmage's lip curled into a sneer. "At the head of a doomed rebellion? Surrounded by peasants and idealists playing at war?" His gaze shifted to Darius. "And traitors, it seems."

Darius stepped forward, placing himself between Lyra and Calidus. "The only traitor here is you. To the people of Aethoria, to everything the Vanguard was supposed to stand for."

"Spare me your righteousness, boy," Calidus spat. "You have no idea of the forces at play here." He turned back to Lyra. "But you... you could. Join me, child. Together, we could remake Aethoria into something truly great."

Lyra's eyes narrowed. "I've seen your version of 'greatness.' I'll pass."

Calidus sighed, a look of genuine regret crossing his features. "Then you leave me no choice." He raised his hand, magic crackling at his fingertips. "Surrender now, and I will spare your followers. Resist, and I'll turn this hill into a graveyard."

Time seemed to slow as Lyra considered her options. She could see the fear in her people's eyes, hear the whispers of doubt rippling through their ranks. But beneath it all, a current of determination, of hope.

"Never," Lyra said, her voice ringing with conviction. She stretched out her hand, channeling every ounce of power she possessed.

A bolt of pure energy erupted from her palm and slammed into Calidus' chest. The Archmage's eyes widened in surprise as he was thrown backward, his form shimmering and dissolving.

"An illusion," Darius breathed. "He's not really here."

As if in response to his words, Calidus' disembodied voice echoed around them. "Impressive, child. But not enough. You have one hour to consider my offer. After that... well, I hope you've made peace with your gods."

The magical barrier dissipated with a thunderous crack, leaving an eerie silence in its wake.

Lyra turned to her assembled forces, seeing the mixture of fear and determination on their faces. "You heard him," she shouted. "One hour to prepare. Make every second count!"

As the rebels scrambled to shore up their defenses, Lyra felt a hand on her arm. Darius pulled her aside, his expression grave.

"We need to talk," he said. "Privately."

Lyra nodded and followed him to a secluded corner of the fortress. For a moment, neither spoke, the weight of unspoken words hanging between them.

"Lyra, I..." Darius began, just as Lyra said, "Darius, we-"

They both trailed off, a nervous laugh escaping Lyra's lips. "You first," she said.

Darius took a deep breath. "Lyra, what I'm about to say... I should have said a long time ago. But I was afraid. Afraid of my own feelings, afraid of complicating things." He met her gaze, his eyes intense. "I love you."

The words hit Lyra like a physical force. Joy and fear warred within her as she realized she'd longed to hear those words, even as she feared them.

"Darius," she whispered, her voice thick with emotion. "I love you too. I think I have since the moment we met in that clearing."

For a heartbeat, the world fell away. There was no impending battle, no weight of destiny. Just two people finally admitting what they'd both known for so long.

Then reality returned. Lyra stepped back and wrapped her arms around herself. "But we can't. You know we can't."

Darius' face fell, but he nodded. "I know. You are the rightful Queen of Aethoria. And I'm... I'm a former Vanguard mage with a target on my back."

"It's more than that," Lyra said, her voice breaking. "This war, this fight... it's bigger than us. We can't let our personal feelings get in the way of what needs to be done."

"And what if what needs to be done is for us to be together?" Darius challenged. "What if our love is the key to restoring balance to Aethoria?"

Lyra's heart ached at the hope in his voice. "Or what if it's the thing that destroys everything we've fought for? Darius, think about it. If the people knew, if they thought I was choosing you over the kingdom-"

"They would think you were choosing love over duty," Darius finished. "And in their eyes, that would make you unfit to rule."

Lyra nodded, tears stinging her eyes. "We must put Aethoria first. No matter how much it hurts."

Darius stepped closer and cupped her face in his hands. "Then let me make you a promise. Here and now. When this is over, when Aethoria is free and you sit on the throne you were born to sit on... I will be there. Not as your lover, but as your most loyal subject. Your friend. Whatever you need me to be."

A sob escaped Lyra's throat. She leaned into his touch, remembering the feel of his skin against hers. "And I promise you this. No matter what happens, no matter where this war takes us... you will always have my heart."

Their lips met in a kiss that was both tender and desperate. A goodbye, a promise, a moment snatched from the jaws of fate.

When they finally parted, Lyra steeled herself, pushing down the pain in her chest. "We should go back. There's a battle to prepare for."

Darius nodded, his eyes shining with unshed tears. "For Aethoria," he said quietly.

"For Aethoria," Lyra echoed.

As they emerged from their secluded corner, a commotion near the main gate caught their attention. Aren's voice rose above the din.

"We have movement! The vanguard is advancing!"

Lyra's heart sank. She turned to Darius and saw her own fear and determination reflected in his eyes.

"So much for our hour," she said grimly.

Darius' hand went to the hilt of his sword. "Whatever comes, we will face it together."

Lyra nodded and squared her shoulders. As she moved to take her place at the head of her ragtag army, she felt the weight of the Crown of Whispers more than ever.

The air crackled with magical energy as both sides prepared for battle. Lyra raised her voice, letting it carry over the fortress.

"Stand ready! For Aethoria! For freedom!"

The cry was echoed by hundreds of voices, a roar of defiance in the face of overwhelming odds.

As the first volley of Vanguard spells struck their defenses, Lyra took one last look at Darius. In that moment, she saw all the might-have-beens, all the futures they would never have.

Then she turned her gaze to the enemy, magic coursing through her veins. Whatever the cost, whatever the sacrifice, she would see this through.

For Aethoria. For her people. For a future worth fighting for.

The battle for the soul of the realm had begun.

THIRTEEN
BATTLE LINES

The world exploded in chaos. Vanguard spells slammed into the Rebel defenses, shattering stone and sending splinters of wood flying. Lyra threw up a magical barrier, deflecting a barrage of energy bolts that would have decimated their front line.

"Hold fast!" she shouted, her voice carrying over the din of battle. "Don't let them breach the wall!"

Aren appeared at her side, his sword already slick with blood. "We can't keep this up forever," he panted. "There are too many of them."

A Vanguard soldier scaled the barricade. Lyra spun, unleashing a blast of pure power that sent him flying back into his comrades. "We will hold as long as we can," she said grimly. "Every moment we resist is a moment they grow weaker."

Across the battlefield, she caught sight of Darius. He moved like a whirlwind, his magic intertwining with his swordplay in a deadly dance. For a heartbeat, their eyes locked. A world of unspoken words passed between them before the tide of battle tore them apart again.

"Lyra!" Mira's panicked voice cut through the chaos. "They're breaking through on the east side!"

Lyra's heart raced as she sprinted across the walls. She arrived to find a section of their defenses crumbling, Vanguard troops pouring through the gap.

Without thinking, she thrust out her hands. Power surged through her, unlike anything she'd ever felt before. The very air seemed to ripple as a wave of blue energy erupted from her palms.

The Vanguard soldiers were thrown backward, their weapons and armor disintegrating upon contact with the strange force. The ground beneath their feet buckled and warped, forming an impassable chasm.

Lyra staggered, her vision blurred. Mira caught her before she could fall.

"By the old gods," the young mage whispered. "How did you do that?"

Lyra shook her head, trying to clear the fog from her mind. "I don't know. It was like... like the magic was using me, not the other way around."

Before Mira could answer, a blast of horn cut through the air. Lyra's blood ran cold as she recognized the signal.

"No," she breathed.

The rebel lines parted as a figure stepped onto the battlefield. Archmage Calidus, his robes pristine despite the carnage around him, his eyes fixed on Lyra with predatory intensity.

"Enough of this foolishness," his voice boomed, magically amplified to reach every corner of the battlefield. "Surrender now, Princess, and I will spare what's left of your pitiful army."

Lyra straightened, forcing steel into her spine. "Never," she shouted back. "As long as one of us draws breath, we will resist your tyranny."

Calidus' lips curled into a sneer. "So be it."

He raised his hands, and the air grew heavy with power. Lyra braced herself, drawing on every ounce of magic she possessed.

Her spells collided in a blinding flash of light. The shockwave knocked friend and foe alike off their feet, leaving only Lyra and Calidus standing.

For a moment, neither moved. Then Calidus chuckled, a sound that sent shivers down Lyra's spine.

"Impressive," he said. "You have grown stronger than I expected. But you are still a child, playing with powers you cannot comprehend."

He flicked his wrist, and a tendril of dark energy shot out. Lyra dodged, but not fast enough. Pain scorched her arm, leaving a smoking gash.

"You see?" Calidus taunted. "You are outmatched, girl. Surrender the Crown of Whispers and I may yet show mercy."

Lyra gritted her teeth against the pain. "You want the crown?" She grabbed the delicate circlet from her forehead. "Come and get it."

With all her strength, she threw the crown into the air. Calidus' eyes widened in surprise, his concentration broken for a crucial moment.

Lyra took her chance. She reached out, not with her hands, but with her essence. The crown froze in midair, pulsing with blue light.

Time seemed to slow. Lyra saw the battle raging around her as if from a great distance. She saw Darius fighting his way toward her, desperation in his eyes. She saw Aren rallying the rebel forces, his voice hoarse from shouting. She saw Mira, her young face a mask of awe and fear.

And she saw Calidus, his mask of confidence slipping away as he realized what was happening.

Lyra closed her eyes, surrendering to the magic coursing through her veins. The Crown of Whispers sang to her, a melody as old as Aethoria itself.

When she opened her eyes, the world was different. The crown no longer floated in the air, but sat on her forehead, its power fully awakened. Blue energy crackled around her, lifting her feet off the ground.

"Impossible," Calidus breathed.

Lyra's voice echoed with the weight of centuries as she spoke. "You wanted to see the true power of the Valenwood line, Calidus? Well, here it is."

She thrust out her hands, and raw magic erupted from her palms. It struck Calidus with the force of a tidal wave, sending him flying across the battlefield. He hit the ground hard, his perfectly manicured appearance shattered.

The Vanguard forces, seeing their leader fall, began to waver. The rebels, emboldened by Lyra's display of power, pressed their advantage.

But Lyra barely noticed. The magic surged through her, wild and untamed. She tried to contain it, to gain control, but it was like trying to hold back the ocean.

"Lyra!" Darius' voice cut through the roar of power in her ears. He struggled to her side, his eyes wide with a mixture of awe and fear. "Lyra, you have to stop! It's too much!"

She wanted to answer him, to tell him that she couldn't stop even if she wanted to. But the words wouldn't come. The magic was consuming her, burning away everything she was.

Darius reached for her, but a bolt of energy struck him, knocking him back. "Lyra, please!" he cried. "Remember who you are! Remember what we're fighting for!"

His words pierced the fog of power. Lyra blinked and focused on Darius' face. The love and fear in his eyes.

With a monumental effort, she began to pull back the magic. It fought her, wild and primal, but she was stronger. She was Lyra Valenwood, the rightful heir to the throne of Aethoria. And she would not be controlled.

Slowly, painfully, the surging power receded. Lyra's feet touched the ground and the blue aura around her faded.

For a moment, the battlefield was silent. Then a cheer rose from the rebel ranks. Lyra swayed, exhaustion hitting her like a physical blow. Darius caught her before she could fall.

"I've got you," he murmured. "It's over. We've won."

Lyra wanted to believe him. But as her eyes swept the battlefield, taking in the carnage, the broken bodies of friend and foe alike, she wasn't so sure.

And then she saw him. Calidus, battered but alive, staggered to his feet. Their eyes met across the battlefield, and Lyra saw something in the Archmage's gaze she'd never expected.

Fear.

Without a word, Calidus raised his hand. A swirl of dark energy enveloped him, and he vanished.

The remaining vanguard forces, seeing their leader flee, threw down their weapons. Shouts of surrender echoed across the battlefield.

Lyra collapsed in Darius' arms, the enormity of what had just happened crashing down upon her. They had won the battle, yes. But at what cost?

As the rebels began to secure their prisoners and tend to the wounded, Aren approached. His face was grim, his armor splattered with blood.

"This is not over," he said, his voice low. "Calidus will return. And next time he'll bring everything he's got."

Lyra nodded wearily. "I know. But we'll be ready."

She straightened, forcing strength into her voice as she addressed the assembled rebels. "Today we struck a blow for freedom. For justice. But our struggle is far from over. Calidus and the Vanguard will return, and we must be prepared."

A murmur of agreement rippled through the crowd. Lyra saw determination in their eyes, mixed with a new emotion: hope.

"Rest now," she continued. "Care for our wounded, honor our fallen. Tomorrow we will plan our next move."

As the crowd dispersed, Darius leaned in close. "What are you thinking?" he asked quietly.

Lyra's hand went to the Crown of Whispers, its power a constant hum in the back of her mind. "I think it's time we took the fight to them. No more hiding, no more running."

She met his gaze and saw her own determination reflected in it. "It's time to reclaim my throne."

The words hung in the air, heavy with promise and danger. As the sun began to set on the blood-soaked battlefield, Lyra knew that everything was about to change.

The true war for the soul of Aethoria had just begun.

FOURTEEN
POWER UNLEASHED

The air crackled with arcane energy as Lyra stood atop the crumbling walls of the rebel stronghold. Below, the Vanguard forces surged forward in endless waves, their armor glinting in the harsh sunlight.

"We can't hold them off much longer!" Aren shouted, his voice barely audible over the din of battle. Blood streaked his face, his sword notched and stained.

Lyra gritted her teeth and channelled another burst of magic through the Crown of Whispers. A wave of blue energy rippled outward, sending a group of advancing soldiers flying backward.

"We have to," she panted, her limbs shaking with exhaustion. "If we fall here, all of Aethoria will fall with us."

A horn blast cut through the chaos, its low note sending shivers down Lyra's spine. The lines of the vanguard parted to reveal a figure striding forward with casual arrogance.

Archmage Calidus.

"Your Majesty," Aren's voice was tight with fear. "You cannot face him alone. Let me..."

"No," Lyra cut him off. "Get our people to safety. I'll deal with Calidus."

Aren hesitated, the conflict clear on his face. Then he nodded sharply. "Do not die," he said gruffly, before turning to rally the remaining defenders.

Lyra took a deep breath and squared her shoulders as she descended to meet her nemesis. The battle seemed to pause around her, rebels and Vanguard alike watching with bated breath.

Calidus smiled as she approached, the expression never reaching his cold eyes. "Princess Lyra," he said, his voice carrying easily over the battlefield. "How kind of you to save me the trouble of hunting you down."

"I'm not running anymore, Calidus," Lyra replied, forcing steel into her voice. "This ends today."

The Archmage's smile widened. "On that, my dear, we are in complete agreement."

Without warning, he struck with a bolt of dark energy. Lyra barely managed to deflect it, the force of the impact knocking her backward.

She retaliated with a barrage of magical projectiles, each glowing with the blue light of her awakened power. Calidus weaved between them with inhuman grace, his own magic blazing around him.

"Is that the best you can do?" he taunted. "I expected more from the last of the Valenwood line."

Anger flared in Lyra's chest. She reached deeper, drawing on the well of power that had awakened within her. The Crown of Whispers hummed, its energy intertwining with her own.

The very air around her seemed to warp as she unleashed a torrent of pure magical power. Calidus' eyes widened in surprise. He hurriedly raised a shield, but it shattered under the onslaught. The Archmage was thrown backward, crashing through the ranks of his own soldiers.

There was silence for a moment. Then a cheer rose from the rebel ranks.

Lyra allowed herself a small smile. But their victory was short-lived.

Calidus rose from the wreckage, his pristine robes now tattered and scorched. Gone was the mask of civility. Fury twisted his features as he stalked forward.

"Enough games," he growled. "You want to see real power? Let me show you what it means to control the forces of creation!"

He raised his hands, and the sky darkened. Thunderclouds gathered with unnatural speed, lightning crackling between them. The ground shook beneath their feet.

Lyra's heart raced. She'd never seen magic of this magnitude before. How could she hope to keep up?

As if in answer to her doubt, the Crown of Whispers pulsed. Lyra gasped as knowledge flooded her mind - generations of Valenwood monarchs, their triumphs and failures, their hopes and fears. And through it all, a single truth:

The magic of Aethoria itself coursed through her veins.

Lyra closed her eyes and reached out, not with her hands, but with her very being. She felt the land respond - the roots deep beneath the earth, the wind whispering through the leaves, the steady heartbeat of the ancient mountains.

When she opened her eyes, they blazed with blue fire.

Calidus hesitated, a flicker of uncertainty crossing his face. "What are you..."

Lyra didn't give him a chance to finish. She thrust her hands into the sky, and the elements answered her call. Vines erupted from the ground, ensnaring the Vanguard soldiers. The wind howled, becoming a tempest that scattered their ranks.

And at the center of it all stood Lyra, wrapped in blue flame, the power of Aethoria itself flowing through her.

"Impossible," Calidus breathed.

Lyra met his gaze, her voice resonating with otherworldly power. "You tried to control the magic of this land, Calidus. But you never understood it. It is not meant to be controlled. It is meant to be nurtured, protected."

She took a step forward, and the earth itself seemed to ripple beneath her feet. "I am the rightful heir to the throne of Aethoria. And in the name of my people, I cast you out!"

She brought her hands together in a thunderous clap. A shockwave of pure magical energy exploded outward. Calidus screamed as it struck him, his own dark magic shattering like glass.

The Archmage was lifted from his feet and hurled backward with such force that he disappeared over the horizon.

As suddenly as it had begun, the magical storm subsided. Lyra swayed, the enormity of what she'd done crashing down on her. She would have fallen had not a strong pair of arms caught her.

She looked up, her heart leaping at the familiar face. "Darius?"

He smiled, his eyes shining with a mixture of awe and pride. "I leave you alone for five minutes and you decide to reshape the face of Aethoria?"

Lyra managed a weak laugh. "What can I say? I got bored." Her expression sobered as she took in his condition - his Vanguard uniform torn and bloodied, a fresh scar on his cheek. "You came back."

Darius nodded, his arms tightening around her. "I told you I would. My place is here, Lyra. With you. With our people."

"Our people?" She raised an eyebrow.

"Your people," he corrected. "But I hope... I hope I can still be a part of it. Of your future."

Before Lyra could answer, a commotion from the rebel lines caught her attention. Aren pushed through the crowd, his eyes widening as he took in the scene before him.

"Your Majesty," he said, falling to his knees. Around him, rebels and even some of the surviving Vanguard followed suit. "The day is ours. What are your orders?"

Lyra straightened, aware of the weight of the moment. Of the Crown of Whispers on her forehead and the expectations of an entire kingdom on her shoulders.

"Tend to the wounded," she said, her voice carrying across the battlefield. "Friend and foe alike. And prepare to march. It is time to reclaim our capital."

A cheer went up from the assembled troops. As they dispersed to carry out their orders, Lyra turned back to Darius.

"You asked if you could be a part of this future," she said quietly. "The truth is, I can't imagine that future without you in it."

Darius' smile was brighter than the sun. He leaned in, their lips meeting in a kiss that held all the promise of tomorrow.

But as they parted, a shiver ran down Lyra's spine. She looked to the horizon, where Calidus had vanished.

"He's still out there," she muttered.

Darius nodded grimly. "And he won't stop until he's destroyed everything we fought for."

Lyra squared her shoulders, her resolve hardening. "Then we'll be ready. Whatever comes next, we will face it together."

As the sun began to set on the battlefield, casting long shadows across the war-torn land, Lyra couldn't shake the feeling that this was only the beginning.

The true test of her strength, her leadership, and her heart still lay ahead.

And the fate of Aethoria hung in the balance.

FIFTEEN
AFTERMATH OF BETRAYAL

Steel rang against steel as Lyra parried another strike, her arms trembling with exhaustion. The rebel camp burned around her, tents collapsing in sheets of flame. Screams of the wounded mingled with the clash of battle.

"Your Majesty!" Aren's voice cut through the chaos. "The eastern perimeter's breached!"

Lyra spun, the Crown of Whispers flaring as she deflected an incoming spell. The magical backlash sent her attacker sprawling, but three more Vanguard soldiers took his place. Too many. They were everywhere.

And it was all Thorne's fault.

The betrayal burned hotter than the fires consuming their camp. Her mentor, her advisor, her friend – all those years of guidance had been nothing but careful manipulation. Each memory now tainted by the knowledge that he'd been Calidus's creature all along.

"Fall back!" she commanded, raising a magical barrier to cover the retreat of a group of wounded rebels. "Get to the caves!"

But even as she gave the order, she knew it was too late. The Vanguard had positioned troops at every escape route, hemming them in with practiced efficiency. Of course, they had – Thorne had told them exactly where to strike.

A familiar figure stepped through the smoke, and Lyra's heart clenched. Thorne stood before her, resplendent in Vanguard robes she'd never seen him wear. His weathered face bore an expression of almost paternal regret.

"It didn't have to be this way, child," he said softly. "If you'd only listened—"

"Spare me your false concern," Lyra spat, magic crackling around her clenched fists. "How long? How long have you been feeding information to Calidus?"

"Since the beginning." No hesitation, no shame. Just calm certainty that made her want to scream. "Someone had to guide you to this moment. To help you understand the true power you carry."

Movement in her peripheral vision – Darius working his way closer, trying to flank Thorne without being noticed. She kept talking, holding her former mentor's attention.

"The power I carry?" Her laugh held no humor. "The power you helped Calidus corrupt? The magic you twisted into something monstrous?"

"Monstrous?" Thorne shook his head like a disappointed teacher. "Oh, Lyra. You still don't understand. The Vanguard doesn't corrupt magic – we perfect it. We give it purpose and direction. Without our guidance, wild magic would tear this realm apart."

"You're wrong." The words emerged as a growl. "Magic isn't meant to be controlled. It's meant to be—"

A horn blast cut through the night, its deep note rattling bones. Thorne smiled, and fear bloomed in Lyra's chest.

"Ah," he said. "Right on time."

The ground shook. Through gaps in the burning tents, Lyra saw an impossible silhouette against the starlit sky. A dragon, larger than any in living memory, its scales gleaming like polished obsidian. And on its back...

"Calidus," she breathed.

The Archmage's voice boomed across the battlefield, magically amplified to reach every ear. "Did you think you could hide forever, little queen? That your pathetic rebellion could stand against the might of the Vanguard?"

The dragon landed with earth-shaking force, its wings scattering fire like leaves in a storm. Calidus dismounted with fluid grace, his midnight-blue robes rippling with barely contained power.

"Thorne," he called. "Is she ready?"

"Nearly, my lord." Thorne's eyes never left Lyra's face. "She just needs one final push."

Understanding dawned too late. This wasn't just an attack – it was a trap. They'd been herding her, manipulating her, pushing her toward...

Lyra felt the magic surge before she saw it. Raw power exploded from Thorne's hands, too fast to dodge, too strong to block. She threw up a desperate shield, knowing it wouldn't be enough.

The impact never came.

Darius appeared between them; sword raised, magic blazing. The spell struck and shattered his hastily erected barrier, but those precious seconds were all Lyra needed.

She reached deep inside, to the place where her power mingled with the ancient magic of the crown. Energy coursed through her veins like liquid fire. The Crown of Whispers ignited, bathing the battlefield in azure light.

"Enough!"

The word carried power that made reality itself shudder. A shockwave of pure magic burst from Lyra's core, knocking friend and foe alike to the ground.

"Get them to the caves!" Aren's voice cut through the chaos as he organized the retreat. Rebels who could still walk helped carry the wounded, taking advantage of the devastation Lyra's power had wrought. Through blurring vision, she saw Mira leading a group along the hidden path they'd prepared for just such a disaster. At least some would survive this night.

Only Calidus remained standing, his eyes gleaming with triumph.

"Yes," he breathed. "Show us what you can really do."

Lyra's vision blurred as power continued to pour from her in waves. She could feel the magic responding, not just from within but from the land itself. Trees groaned and swayed. The earth buckled and heaved. Above, storm clouds gathered with unnatural speed.

Her uncontrolled magic had carved a temporary safe zone, the raw power keeping the Vanguard forces at bay. But it wouldn't last. Already she could feel the wild energy beginning to fade, leaving her drained and vulnerable.

"Lyra!" Darius's voice seemed to come from very far away. "You have to control it!"

But she couldn't. The magic now had a will of its own: wild, hungry, and unstoppable. Just as Thorne had planned. Just as Calidus had wanted all along.

The last thing she saw before consciousness fled was the Archmage's satisfied smile.

The real battle for Aethoria's soul was about to begin.

And Lyra had just played right into their hands.

SIXTEEN
SHADOWS OF DOUBT

Pain dragged Lyra back to consciousness. Every heartbeat sent daggers through her skull, and every breath felt like inhaling smoke. She forced her eyes open to find herself in a dimly lit cave, the rough stone ceiling swimming in and out of focus.

"Easy." Mira's face appeared above her, drawn with exhaustion. "The magical backlash nearly killed you."

"Two days," Mira answered her unspoken question. "The magical backlash knocked you unconscious. The Vanguard's been regrouping, dealing with the damage your power caused to their own forces. Thorne convinced Calidus to wait and told him you'd be more vulnerable when you woke."

Lyra tried to sit up, but her body refused to cooperate. "The others?"

"Most made it to the emergency shelters." Mira's hesitation spoke volumes. "We lost seventeen in the attack. Another dozen are missing."

The numbers hit Lyra like physical blows. Seventeen dead.

Because she hadn't seen the betrayal coming. Because she'd trusted blindly.

"Darius?" Her voice cracked on his name.

"Here." He emerged from the shadows, looking as battered as she felt. A hastily bandaged wound on his shoulder showed where he'd taken Thorne's attack. "Though I'd be dead if Aren hadn't pulled me clear when you..." He trailed off.

"When I lost control." The words tasted bitter. She could still feel it – the wild magic surging through her, too vast to contain exactly as Thorne had planned.

Footsteps echoed through the cave. Aren appeared, followed by what remained of her war council. Their faces bore a mixture of concern and something worse – doubt.

"Report," she managed, forcing herself to sit up despite Mira's protests.

"We're secure for now." Aren's clipped tone suggested he was editing heavily. "The Vanguard's pulled back to regroup. But they know where we are. It's only a matter of time."

"They've always known," Lord Garrick said, his mechanical arm whirring as he clenched his fist. "Thorne made sure of that."

The name sent a ripple of tension through the group. Lyra saw hands tighten on weapons and saw the sidelong glances. The seeds of paranoia Thorne had planted were already taking root.

"How can we be sure he was working alone?" someone muttered. "There could be other spies—"

"There aren't." Lyra's voice cut through the whispers. "Thorne didn't need other spies. He had me." The admission scraped her raw. "Every decision I made, every strategy I approved –

he shaped them all. Guided me exactly where Calidus wanted me to go."

"Which raises the question," Lord Garrick said carefully, "of whether you're fit to lead us now."

The cave went deadly silent. Even the torches seemed to hold their breath.

Darius stepped forward, magic crackling around his clenched fists. "You dare question—"

"Let him speak." Lyra's quiet command stopped Darius in his tracks. "Go on, Lord Garrick. Say what needs to be said."

The former Vanguard commander met her gaze steadily. "You lost control of your power today. You nearly killed your own people in the process. And now we learn that our enemies have orchestrated everything you've done. Why should we trust your judgment?"

It was the question Lyra had been asking herself since waking. The question that burned beneath her skin like fever.

"Thorne didn't just betray our location," Lord Garrick said, his voice heavy. "He betrayed our trust in you. Every victory you led us to, every strategy you devised - how do we know they weren't all part of his manipulation?"

She looked around the cave at what remained of her rebellion. Faces scarred by battle and haunted by loss stared back, waiting, judging, ready to fracture at the slightest push.

The Crown of Whispers sat cold and silent on her brow, its power dormant. Or waiting.

"You shouldn't trust my judgment," she said finally. The words rang with quiet conviction. "Trust my actions instead."

She pushed herself to her feet, ignoring the pain that tried to drag her back down. "I've made mistakes. Terrible ones. But everything I've done – everything I will do – is for Aethoria. Not for power or glory or revenge. For our people. For our future."

Her legs trembled, but she forced them to hold. "Thorne and Calidus think they know me. I think they can predict my every move because they shaped who I am. But they're wrong."

Energy stirred within her, different from before. Not the wild torrent that had overwhelmed her, but something steadier. Something that felt like truth.

"They didn't shape who I am," she continued, strength returning to her voice. "You did. All of you. Every battle we've fought together, every loss we've shared, every victory we've celebrated – that's what made me who I am. And that's something they can never understand."

The Crown of Whispers began to warm, its magic resonating with her words.

"So yes, question my judgment. Challenge my decisions. But know this – I will never stop fighting for Aethoria. And I will never, ever let them win."

Silence fell again, but it was different this time. Charged with possibility rather than doubt.

Lord Garrick was the first to move. He drew his sword and laid it at her feet. "The Vanguard taught us that power flows from strength," he said gruffly. "But you've shown us it flows from something else. Something they can't corrupt."

One by one, the others followed suit. Not blindly, not without reservation, but with clear eyes and firm resolve.

Aren cleared his throat. "So what now, Your Majesty?"

Lyra looked at Darius and saw her own determination reflected in his eyes. Then to Mira, whose faith had never wavered. To each face in the cave, marked by doubt but choosing to believe anyway.

"Now," she said, "we remind Thorne and Calidus exactly who they're dealing with."

The Crown of Whispers blazed to life, but the magic felt different this time. Controlled. Purposeful. Ready.

"They think they know our weaknesses?" A fierce smile curved her lips. "Let's show them our strength instead."

And in that moment, surrounded by those who chose to follow not out of blind faith but reasoned trust, Lyra felt something shift. The doubt that had plagued her since Thorne's betrayal didn't vanish but transformed – from a weakness into a weapon, from a burden into a shield.

They had tried to break her.

They had failed.

Now, it was her turn.

SEVENTEEN
POWER UNLEASHED

Dawn kissed the mountaintops as Lyra stood at the cave's mouth, watching mist coil through the valley below. The Vanguard camp sprawled across the lowlands, torches dotting the darkness like fallen stars. Somewhere in that maze of tents, Thorne and Calidus waited, confident in their victory.

"The scouts report their defenses are heaviest to the south." Darius stepped beside her, close enough that their shoulders brushed. "They're expecting us to run deeper into the mountains."

"Of course they are." Lyra's fingers traced the rough stone of the cave wall, feeling the ancient magic that pulsed within. "It's what Thorne taught me to do. Always retreat to higher ground."

"Then we do the opposite." Aren materialized from the shadows, his scarred face set with grim determination. "Hit them where they least expect it."

Lyra nodded, the Crown of Whispers warming against her

skin. "Exactly. Thorne thinks he knows every move I'll make. Time to show him how wrong he is."

She turned to face the assembled rebels – fewer now than before, but their eyes burned with a fierce resolve that mere numbers couldn't match. These weren't just followers anymore. They were survivors. Warriors. Family.

Lyra looked at her gathered forces - tempered by survival. They'd lost good people in the camp attack, but those who remained had seen her at her worst and chosen to stay anyway. More importantly, they'd seen what raw magic could do when unleashed.

"Last time, I lost control," she told them. "This time, we use that power with purpose."

"The plan is simple," she said, her voice carrying to every corner of the cave. "While they watch the mountain passes, we strike at their heart. No elaborate strategies, no clever feints. Just pure, overwhelming force."

"They outnumber us three to one," Lord Garrick pointed out, though his tone held more curiosity than doubt.

"They do." Lyra's smile was sharp as a blade. "But they don't have what we have."

She reached out with her magic, letting them feel what she'd discovered during her communion with the mountain: the ancient power that dwelled in stone and earth, waiting to be awakened. It was wild magic but not chaotic—primal and purposeful like nature itself.

Mira gasped as understanding dawned. "The ley lines. They run right under their camp."

"The very same lines they've been trying to control and corrupt." Lyra's power pulsed in time with the earth's heartbeat. "Time to show them what happens when you try to cage something that was meant to be free."

The rebels moved into position as the first light of true dawn painted the sky. They would have only one chance at this. One moment to prove that everything they'd lost, everything they'd sacrificed, hadn't been in vain.

Lyra felt Darius's hand slip into hers. She squeezed it, drawing strength from his touch.

"Whatever happens," he murmured, "I'm with you."

She met his gaze and saw everything they'd left unsaid shining in his eyes. "I know."

"He'll expect another magical storm," Darius said quietly. "After what happened at the camp..."

"Good." Lyra's fingers traced the crown. "Let him prepare for chaos. He won't expect precision."

The signal came – three sharp whistles cutting through the morning mist. Lyra closed her eyes and reached deep, not just into her own power but into the very bones of the earth. The Crown of Whispers blazed to life, no longer a weight but an amplifier, focusing her will into something greater than herself.

Magic answered her call. Not the refined, controlled power the Vanguard praised, but something older. Something that I remembered when mountains were young and magic ran wild and free.

The ground began to shake.

In the valley below, shouts of alarm rose from the Vanguard camp. Lyra opened her eyes to see chaos erupting as the earth itself rebelled against their presence. Tents collapsed as the ground buckled and heaved. Fissures opened, swallowing supply wagons and weapons caches.

"Now!" she commanded.

The rebels surged forward, taking advantage of the confusion. Aren led the first wave, his sword gleaming as it cut through the morning mist. Lord Garrick commanded the second, mechanical arm whirring as he directed precise strikes at key positions.

But it was Mira who truly shone. The young mage had gathered other magic-sensitive rebels, forming them into a coordinated unit that turned the Vanguard's own defenses against them. Wards shattered. Magical barriers collapsed. The very air crackled with unleashed power.

Through it all, Lyra maintained her connection to the ley lines, directing their power with a precision that would have seemed impossible days ago. Every surge of energy, every tremor and eruption served a purpose. Not to destroy, but to disrupt. To break the Vanguard's perfect formations and practiced responses.

"Impressive." The voice cut through the chaos like a blade of ice. "Though I expected nothing less from my star pupil."

Thorne stood atop a rise, looking exactly as he had in all those years of mentorship. But now Lyra saw him clearly – the calculated stance, the careful manipulation in every gesture.

"You taught me well," she called back, magic coiling around her like a storm about to break. "Perhaps too well."

He shook his head, almost sadly. "You still don't understand. Everything that's happening – even this rebellion – serves a greater purpose. You're playing your part perfectly."

"No." The word carried power that made reality tremble. "I'm done playing parts in other people's stories. This is my choice. My power. My destiny."

She struck with everything she had. Magic exploded from her in a wave of pure force, shattering Thorne's defenses like glass. He staggered, genuine surprise flickering across his face before her second attack sent him flying.

But even as he fell, a shadow passed overhead. The dragon's roar shook the valley as Calidus descended from above, dark magic swirling around him like a cloak.

"Enough games," the Archmage snarled. "If you won't be guided, you'll be broken."

Power beyond anything Lyra had ever felt slammed into her magical shields. The Crown of Whispers screamed in her mind as she fought to hold back the assault. Darkness crept in at the edges of her vision.

Then Darius was there, his magic joining with hers. Mira appeared on her other side, then others – rebels and reformed Vanguard alike, lending their strength to her cause.

And beneath it all, the ley lines pulsed. Ancient. Patient. Waiting for her command.

Lyra looked up at Calidus, seeing not the terrifying figure of her nightmares but a man desperately trying to control forces beyond his understanding.

"You're right," she said, her voice carrying despite the magical maelstrom. "Enough games."

She opened herself fully to the wild magic, not trying to direct it but simply serving as a conduit for its power. The Crown of Whispers flared like a newborn star.

The world went white.

When Lyra's vision cleared, the valley had been transformed. Much of the Vanguard camp lay in ruins, its remains scattered across the changed landscape. New stone formations thrust up from the earth, glowing with residual magic.

But something was wrong. The magic had taken too much from her. Black spots danced at the edges of her vision as she swayed on her feet.

"Lyra!" Darius lunged to catch her as her knees buckled.

A shadow passed overhead. Through blurring vision, she saw Calidus rise from the wreckage, dark magic swirling around him like a storm. His dragon circled lower, its wings stirring up clouds of dust and debris.

"Now you see," the Archmage's voice boomed across the valley. "This is what happens when you channel power beyond your understanding."

Lyra tried to stand, to fight, but her body wouldn't respond. She'd pushed too far, too fast. The Crown of Whispers sat cold and silent on her brow.

"Your Majesty, we have to retreat!" Aren shouted, already organizing a defensive line. But they were exposed, scattered across the transformed battlefield.

Calidus raised his hands. Dark energy crackled between his fingers. "The time for games is over."

The spell hit like a physical blow. Darius's shield shattered. Lyra felt herself torn from his grasp, pulled upward by invisible forces. The last thing she heard was his desperate cry as darkness claimed her.

"Take the survivors to the Spire," Calidus commanded as Lyra's limp form floated to his dragon's back. "It's time our queen learned the true price of defiance."

Through the gathering dark, Lyra sensed more than saw Thorne rise from where she'd thrown him. "And what of the others, my lord?"

"Let them run." Calidus's voice held cruel amusement. "They'll come for her. And when they do..."

Consciousness fled before she could hear the rest. But as the dragon bore her away, a single thought burned through the darkness:

This wasn't over. Not while she still drew breath.

The real battle was just beginning.

EIGHTEEN
BROKEN TRUST

The cave echoed with the clash of steel and panicked screams. Lyra sprinted through the winding tunnels, her heart pounding in her ears. The Crown of Whispers pulsed on her forehead, its magic responding to her need.

She burst into the main chamber and found chaos. Rebels were battling Vanguard soldiers who seemed to materialize from the shadows. How had they broken through their defenses so quickly?

"Lyra!" Darius' voice cut through the noise. He fought his way to her side, his sword slick with blood. "We have to get you out of here. The entire cave system is at risk."

She shook her head, magic crackling at her fingertips. "I will not abandon our people."

A Vanguard soldier lunged at her. Lyra thrust her hand out, a surge of power sending him flying back into the fray.

Aren appeared, his face grim. "Your Majesty, Darius is right. We can't hold them off much longer. We must retreat."

Lyra opened her mouth to argue, but a familiar voice stopped her.

"Oh, I don't think you're going anywhere."

The fighting seemed to pause as all eyes turned to the cave entrance. Archmage Calidus stood there, resplendent in his Vanguard robes. And beside him...

"Thorne?" Lyra breathed, disbelief coursing through her.

The old man's face was a mask of regret, tinged with determination. "I'm sorry, Lyra. But this ends now."

The betrayal hit Lyra like a physical blow. She staggered back, her mind reeling. "How... why?"

Calidus smiled, the expression never reaching his cold eyes. "Come now, Princess. Did you really think your little rebellion had a chance? Thorne was my eyes and ears from the beginning."

"You're lying," Darius growled, stepping protectively in front of Lyra.

Thorne shook his head. "He is not. I've served the Vanguard for years. Waiting, watching, guiding events to this very moment."

Lyra's world tilted on its axis. Every memory, every moment of trust and companionship with Thorne, now tainted by this revelation.

"Why?" she demanded, her voice breaking. "After all we've been through, all we've fought for..."

"Because it's the only way to save Aethoria," Thorne replied, his eyes pleading for understanding. "The old ways are dying, Lyra. The magic is fading. Only the Vanguard has the power to keep our kingdom from crumbling to dust."

Calidus nodded in agreement. "You see? Even your most trusted advisor knows the truth. Join us, Lyra. With your power, we can usher in a new age of prosperity for Aethoria."

Lyra's hand went to the Crown of Whispers. Its magic surged, responding to her excitement. She looked around the chamber and saw the fear and confusion on the faces of her people.

"Never," she spat. "I will die before I let you twist the magic of this land for your own gain."

Calidus sighed dramatically. "Such a waste. Very well, then. Thorne, if you would?"

The old man stepped forward, his hands raised. Magic shimmered in the air around him, more powerful than Lyra had ever seen him use.

"I am truly sorry, my dear," he said softly. "But this is bigger than any of us."

He brought his hands together with a thunderous clap. A shockwave of energy exploded outward, hitting rebels and Vanguard alike. Lyra hurriedly threw up a shield, but the force still knocked her back.

As the dust settled, she saw Thorne and Calidus advancing, Vanguard soldiers falling in behind them.

"Retreat!" Aren's voice boomed through the chamber. "Everyone to the rear tunnels!"

The rebels began to fall back, helping the wounded as they went. Lyra stood her ground, magic crackling around her.

"Lyra, come on!" Darius tugged at her arm. "We can't win this fight. Not here, not now."

She struggled for a moment, locked in a battle of wills with Calidus. Then, with a cry of frustration, she turned and ran.

They sprinted through twisting corridors, the sounds of pursuit echoing behind them. Lyra's mind raced. How many of her secrets had Thorne revealed? How long had he been feeding information to the Vanguard?

They emerged into a small cave where a group of rebels had gathered. Mira rushed to Lyra's side, her face pale with fear.

"What happened?" she asked. "How did they find us?"

Lyra's throat tightened. "Thorne. He... he betrayed us."

A collective gasp came from the assembled rebels. Mira's eyes widened in disbelief.

"No," she whispered. "It can't be."

Aren pushed through the crowd, his expression grim. "We need to keep moving. There's an old mining tunnel leading out of the mountains. If we can reach it-"

A tremor shook the cave, dust and small rocks raining down from the ceiling.

"They're collapsing the tunnels," Darius realized aloud. "Trying to trap us."

Panic swept through the group. Lyra raised her voice, forcing a calm she didn't feel into her tone.

"Everyone, stay together. We'll get through this. Aren, lead the way. Darius and I will bring up the rear."

As the rebels left, Lyra caught Mira's arm. "I'm sorry," she said softly. "For suspecting you before. I should have known..."

Mira cut her off with a quick hug. "It's okay. You did what you had to do. Now let's get out of here."

They started down the tunnel, the sounds of pursuit growing louder behind them. Lyra's mind whirled with possibilities, each more desperate than the last. How could they escape? Where could they go that the vanguard wouldn't find them?

Another tremor shook the corridor. Cracks sprawled across the ceiling, rocks and debris raining down on them.

"Move!" Darius shouted, shoving Lyra ahead of him.

They sprinted through the collapsing tunnel, dodging falling rocks and leaping over widening cracks in the floor. The air filled with dust, making it hard to breathe, hard to see.

A scream pierced the chaos. Lyra skidded to a halt and turned to see a young rebel trapped under a fallen boulder. Without thinking, she lunged back.

"Lyra, no!" Darius called after her.

Ignoring him, she reached the trapped rebel. The girl's face was pale with pain and fear.

"Help me!" Lyra yelled to the others.

Aren and Darius were at her side in an instant. Together they pressed against the boulder. It didn't budge.

Lyra closed her eyes and reached for the magic within her. The Crown of Whispers hummed, its power coursing through her veins. She placed her hands on the boulder and pushed, not with her muscles, but with pure magical power.

The rock lifted and floated in the air. Aren and Darius quickly pulled the girl free. As soon as she was free, Lyra released her grip. The boulder crashed back down, sending tremors through the unstable passage.

"We have to go," Aren urged, supporting the injured rebel. "Now!"

They ran on, the tunnel seeming endless. Lyra's lungs burned, her legs ached, but she pushed through the pain. Behind them, the sound of pursuit grew louder.

Finally, they broke out into the open. The night sky stretched above them, stars twinkling coldly. But there was no time for relief.

"There!" Mira pointed to a narrow path that wound down the mountainside. "If we can reach the forest below, we can lose them."

They half ran, half slid down the treacherous path. Loose rocks clattered beneath their feet, threatening to send them tumbling into the abyss.

A shout from above signaled that their pursuers had emerged from the cave. Arrows whistled past, uncomfortably close.

"Keep going!" Lyra shouted. "Don't stop!"

They reached the tree line and plunged into the darkness of the forest. Branches whipped at their faces as they ran, roots threatened to trip them at every step.

After what seemed like hours, Aren called a halt. They gathered in a small clearing, chests heaving as they struggled to catch their breath.

"I think... I think we lost them," Mira panted.

Lyra did a quick headcount. Her heart sank as she realized how few of them had made it out. Barely two dozen, out of the hundreds that had been in the rebel camp.

"What now?" someone asked, their voice shaking with exhaustion and fear.

All eyes turned to Lyra. She straightened, forcing strength into her voice despite the despair that threatened to overwhelm her.

"We will regroup. We find a safe place to rest and tend to our wounded. And then..." She paused, the weight of her situation crashing down on her. "Then we figure out our next move."

Darius stepped closer, his voice low. "Lyra, I hate to say this, but... is there a next move? The Vanguard knows all our plans, all our hiding places. We have no supplies, no weapons. How can we continue?"

The question hung in the air, heavy with implication. Lyra looked around at the faces of her people - tired, frightened, but still looking to her for guidance.

She thought of Thorne's betrayal, of the lives lost, of the seemingly insurmountable odds they faced. For a moment, the temptation to give up, to surrender, was almost overwhelming.

Then her hand went to the Crown of Whispers. Its steady pulse reminded her of who she was, what she was fighting for.

"We continue because we must," she said, her voice growing stronger. "Because the moment we give up, Calidus wins. And I, for one, am not willing to let that happen."

A murmur of agreement rippled through the group. Aren nodded in agreement, while Mira's eyes glowed with renewed determination.

Darius studied her face for a long moment before a small smile tugged at his lips. "So, Your Majesty," he said, "what are your orders?"

Lyra took a deep breath, her mind already forming plans. "Aren, take a team and scout the area. Find us a defensible place to set up camp. Mira, take care of the wounded as best you can with what we have."

As the others moved to carry out her orders, Darius remained at her side. "And what about you?" he asked quietly.

Lyra's hand tightened on the Crown of Whispers. "I'm going to find out how to use this power, once and for all. No more holding back, no more fear. It's time for me to fully embrace my heritage."

Darius nodded, understanding and a hint of concern in his eyes. "I'll be here with you. Whatever comes next."

As the remnants of her rebel force prepared for an uncertain future, Lyra looked to the stars above. Somewhere out there, Calidus and his vanguard were plotting their next move. And this time, she vowed, she would be ready.

The road ahead was dark and fraught with danger. But as long as they had each other, as long as they had hope, they had a chance.

And sometimes one chance was all it took to change the world.

NINETEEN
LOVE OR DUTY

The makeshift rebel camp huddled in the shade of ancient trees, a patchwork of tattered tents and exhausted survivors. Lyra sat alone at its edge, her eyes fixed on the horizon where the first hints of dawn were painting the sky. The Crown of Whispers rested in her lap, its blue glow fading to a faint pulse.

Footsteps approached, and Lyra tensed before she recognized the familiar tread.

"You should rest," Darius said quietly, settling down beside her.

Lyra shook her head. "I can't sleep. Every time I close my eyes, I see..." She trailed off, unable to articulate the horrors that plagued her dreams.

Darius's hand found hers, a warm anchor in the cold morning air. "We made it out. Thanks to you."

"But at what cost?" Lyra's voice cracked. "How many died because I wasn't strong enough? Because I trusted the wrong people?"

"You can't blame yourself for Thorne's betrayal," Darius insisted. "None of us saw it coming."

Lyra pulled her hand away and stood abruptly. "I should have. I'm supposed to be their leader, their queen. And I led them right into Calidus' trap."

Darius rose, his eyes searching her face. "Lyra, you're being too hard on yourself. You..."

"Am I?" She turned to face him, her voice rising. "Look around you, Darius. This is all that's left of our rebellion. A handful of survivors with no supplies, no plan. How are we supposed to fight the Vanguard now?"

Her words hung in the air between them, heavy with despair. Darius took a step closer, his expression intense.

"We fight because we must," he said, echoing her own words from days before. "Because the moment we give up, Calidus wins. Isn't that what you told us?"

Lyra deflated, the fight draining out of her. "I don't know if I believe that anymore."

Darius caught her shoulders, forcing her to meet his gaze. "Then believe in us. In me. Lyra, I-"

"Don't," she cut him off, her heart clenching. "Please, don't say it."

But Darius continued, his voice low and urgent. "I love you. I think I have from the moment we met in that clearing. And I know you feel the same way."

Lyra closed her eyes, fighting back tears. "It doesn't matter how we feel. I have a duty to my people, to Aethoria. I can't put my own desires above that."

"Who says you have to choose?" Darius argued. "Why can't you be both a queen and a woman in love?"

"Because love is a weakness that Calidus will exploit," Lyra shot back. "Because every moment I spend thinking about you is a moment I'm not focused on saving our people."

Darius flinched as if hit. "So that's it? You're just going to push me away?"

Lyra's resolve wavered at the pain in his eyes. She opened her mouth to reply, but a cry from the camp interrupted her.

"Your Majesty! Come quickly!"

They hurried back to find Aren and Mira huddled over a map, their faces grim.

"What is it?" Lyra demanded.

Aren pointed to a spot on the weathered parchment. "Vanguard patrols. They're sweeping the forest, approaching our position."

Lyra's mind raced. "How long do we have?"

"Hours at most," Mira replied. "We have to move."

But where? The question hung unspoken in the air. They all knew that their options were dwindling by the second.

A commotion at the edge of the camp caught their attention. Two rebels were dragging a struggling figure between them.

"Found this one sneaking around the perimeter," one reported. "Says he has a message for you, Your Majesty."

The prisoner raised his head, and Lyra's blood ran cold. She recognized the Vanguard insignia on his tattered uniform.

"Speak," she ordered, her voice harsh.

The soldier's eyes darted nervously between the rebels before settling on Lyra. "Archmage Calidus sends his regards. He says... he says it's time to end this game. Surrender to him by sundown, or he'll raze every village in the Eastern Forests to the ground."

A murmur of horror rippled through the assembled rebels. Lyra's mind whirled with the implications. Thousands of innocent lives held hostage for her capture.

"You lie," Darius snapped, his hand going to the hilt of his sword.

The soldier shook his head furiously. "I swear on my life, it is the truth. The Archmage... he's tired of waiting. He wants the Crown of Whispers, and he'll do anything to get it."

Lyra's hand went to the crown, its magic humming in response to her confusion. She turned to Aren. "Is there any way we can evacuate the villages in time?"

Aren's face was grim. "Not all of them. Not even close."

The weight of the decision pressed down on Lyra like a physical force. She looked around at the faces of her people - tired, frightened, but still looking to her for guidance.

And then there was Darius. His eyes met hers, a silent plea in their depths. Don't do this, they seemed to say. We'll find another way.

But there was no other way. Not this time.

Lyra squared her shoulders and forced steel into her voice. "Prepare to break camp. We move in an hour."

"Where to?" Mira asked.

"The capital," Lyra replied. "I will give Calidus what he wants."

The outcry was immediate. Voices rose in protest, in disbelief, in fear.

"You can't!"

"It's suicide!"

"There must be another way!"

Lyra raised her hand to silence. "I will not sacrifice innocent lives for my own safety. This is the only choice."

"Then I'm coming with you," Darius declared, stepping forward.

Lyra shook her head. "No. I need you here, leading what's left of our forces. If this goes wrong... if Calidus doesn't keep his word... you're their best hope."

"Lyra, please," Darius' voice broke. "Don't do this."

For a moment, Lyra allowed herself to imagine another way. A life where she and Darius could be together, free from the burden of crowns and prophecies. But it was a fantasy, nothing more.

She met his gaze, pouring all her unspoken feelings into that one look. "I'm sorry," she whispered. "But this is who I am. This is what I have to do."

Before he could argue any further, she turned to Aren. "Prepare a small team. We'll leave as soon as we're ready."

As the camp erupted into frantic activity, Lyra retreated to her tent. She sank onto her bedroll, the weight of her decision bearing down on her.

The Crown of Whispers pulsed in her hands, its magic a constant reminder of her fate. She thought of her parents, of the legacy they'd left her. Of the people who counted on her to be the queen they needed.

And she thought of Darius. Of the future they might have had in another life.

A single tear trickled down her cheek as Lyra made her choice. Love or duty. The woman or the queen.

In the end, there was only one path she could take.

As the first rays of sunlight crept over the horizon, Lyra emerged from her tent. The small team she'd chosen was waiting, grim and ready.

Darius stood apart from the others, his eyes never leaving her face. When she approached, he opened his mouth to speak.

Lyra silenced him with a kiss, pouring everything she couldn't say into that one moment. When they parted, both breathless, she pressed her forehead against his.

"If I don't come back," she murmured, "promise me you'll keep fighting. For Aethoria. For our people."

Darius' arms tightened around her. "I promise," he whispered. "But you'll come back. You have to."

Lyra managed a small smile as she stepped back. "Take care of them," she said, loud enough for the others to hear. "That's an order."

Before her resolve could waver, she turned and walked to the edge of the forest. Her small band of rebels fell in behind her, ready to face whatever lay ahead.

As they disappeared into the trees, Lyra didn't look back. She couldn't. To look back was to falter, and she needed every ounce of strength for what was to come.

The true test of her strength, her leadership, and her heart awaited her in the capital.

And the fate of Aethoria hung in the balance.

TWENTY
SIEGE

The rebel stronghold buzzed with activity. Lyra stood atop the hastily repaired walls, her eyes fixed on the horizon where the first glimmers of Vanguard armor caught the morning sun. The Crown of Whispers hummed on her forehead, responding to the tension in the air.

"They're here," Aren's fierce voice cut through her thoughts. He handed her a spyglass, his face etched with worry. "And they brought everything they have."

Lyra lifted the glass to her eye, gasping at the sight. Row upon row of Vanguard soldiers stretched across the plain, their numbers seemingly endless. Siege engines loomed behind them, magical energy crackling around their frames.

"How many?" she asked, lowering the scope.

Aren's jaw clenched. "Too many. We're outnumbered at least ten to one."

A shiver ran down Lyra's spine. She turned to survey her own forces - a ragtag band of rebels and villagers, armed with whatever weapons they could cobble together. Their faces were a mixture of determination and fear as they looked to her for guidance.

"Your Majesty!" Mira's voice rang out as she sprinted along the wall. "Darius says the magical defenses are ready. He needs you in the central tower."

Lyra nodded and squared her shoulders. "Aren, supervise the archers. Make every shot count. We can't waste an arrow."

As she hurried to the tower, the first beats of the Vanguard's war drums echoed across the battlefield. The siege had begun.

Darius stood at the center of a complex array of magical sigils, his face beaded with sweat from the effort of maintaining the protective barriers. He looked up as Lyra entered, relief washing over his features.

"You're here," he said, holding out his hand. "Quickly, we must link our powers. It's the only way to stop them."

Lyra hesitated for a split second, remembering their argument of days before. But there was no time for personal feelings now. She took his hand, gasping as their magic intertwined.

The world seemed to shift, colors more vivid, sounds sharper. She could feel the pulse of the land beneath them, the ebb and flow of magical currents.

"By the old gods," she breathed. "Is that how you see the world?"

Darius managed a small smile. "Something like that. Now, focus. Channel your power through the crown. I'll direct it to strengthen our defenses."

Lyra closed her eyes and reached for the source of magic within her. The Crown of Whispers came to life, its energy merging with her own. She directed the power to Darius, trusting him to shape it as needed.

A huge crash shook the tower. Lyra's eyes flew open as she saw a massive boulder crumble against her magical shield.

"It's working!" Mira shouted from her position by the window. "Their siege weapons can't break through!"

But Lyra could feel the strain on her defenses. Each impact sent shockwaves through her bonded magic, threatening to tear it apart.

"We can't keep this up forever," Darius grunted, his face pale with effort.

As if in response to his words, a horn blast cut through the chaos of battle. Lyra's blood ran cold as she recognized the signal.

"No," she whispered. "It can't be."

But it was. Through the tower window, she saw a figure rise above the vanguard forces, carried aloft by swirling dark magic. Archmage Calidus had entered the fray.

His voice boomed across the battlefield, magically amplified to reach every ear. "Lyra Valenwood! Your rebellion ends today. Surrender the Crown of Whispers or watch your people burn!"

He raised his hands to emphasize his threat. The sky darkened as storm clouds gathered with unnatural speed. Lightning arced between Calidus' fingers, building to a crescendo of deadly power.

"Lyra," Darius' urgent voice snapped them back to the present. "We must break the link. I can hold the defenses, but you must face Calidus."

She met his gaze and saw the fear and determination there. "If we separate, the shields will be weaker. You'll be vulnerable."

"We have no choice," he insisted. "You are the only one who can match its power. Go. I'll keep our people safe."

Lyra's heart clenched at the unspoken words between them. She squeezed his hand once before letting go, immediately missing the connection.

"Be careful," she said quietly.

Darius managed a crooked smile. "You too, Your Majesty."

With one last look back, Lyra raced to the top of the tower. She appeared on the open platform just as Calidus unleashed his attack.

A bolt of pure magical energy, as wide as a house, shot toward the rebel stronghold. Lyra thrust out her hands, summoning every ounce of power she possessed.

The Crown of Whispers blazed with blue fire as a shield of swirling energy materialized before her. Calidus' attack slammed into it with earth-shattering force.

For an instant, the world went white. Lyra screamed as the backlash of power threatened to tear her apart. But she held on, drawing strength from the stones beneath her feet.

When her vision cleared, she saw the impossible. Calidus' bolt had been deflected, carving a massive rift in the earth at the side of the fortress.

A cheer went up from the rebel forces. But Lyra did not have time to celebrate. Calidus was already preparing for another attack.

"Impressive," his voice carried on the wind. "But how long can you keep this up, I wonder? How many lives are you willing to sacrifice for your futile resistance?"

Lyra gritted her teeth, gathering her strength for another defense. But doubt gnawed at her. Calidus was right - she couldn't protect everyone forever. Sooner or later, her powers would fail.

As if sensing her uncertainty, Calidus pressed his advantage. "Join me, Lyra. Together, we could remake Aethoria into something truly great. No more war, no more suffering. Isn't that what you want?"

For a heartbeat, Lyra wavered. The temptation to end it all, to stop the bloodshed, was almost overwhelming.

Then a voice broke through her doubt. Aren, screaming from the walls below. "Do not listen to him, Your Majesty! We believe in you!"

Other voices joined in, a chorus of support rising from her people. Lyra's resolve hardened. She straightened, the Crown of Whispers pulsing in time with her heartbeat.

"You are wrong, Calidus," she shouted, her voice carrying over the battlefield. "True peace cannot be built on tyranny and fear. And I will die before I let you twist the magic of this land for your own gain."

With that, she thrust out her hands. But instead of forming another shield, she reached deep into the earth beneath them. The ground began to tremble as Lyra called upon the ancient power of Aethoria itself.

Calidus' eyes widened in shock as massive roots erupted from the earth, wrapping around Vanguard soldiers and siege engines alike. The land itself rose up in defense of its rightful queen.

For a moment, the tide of battle seemed to turn. But then Calidus rallied, dark magic swirling around him like a storm.

"Enough games," he growled. "If you will not see reason, then you will watch everything you love burn!"

He raised his hands, gathering strength for a devastating attack. Lyra braced herself, knowing she had to intercept it or watch her stronghold be obliterated.

But before either could act, a new sound cut through the chaos. A horn blast, unlike any they'd heard before. Ancient and powerful, it seemed to resonate with the very bones of the earth.

Lyra turned, her heart leaping at the sight on the distant horizon. An army was approaching, banners flapping in the wind. And at its head, a figure she'd thought lost forever.

"It can't be," she breathed.

But it was. Riding at the head of the new force, his armor gleaming in the sun, was her father. King Aldric, presumed dead for years, had returned.

As the rebel forces erupted in cheers of renewed hope, Lyra's mind raced with questions. How had her father survived? Where had he been all this time? And what would his return mean for the future of Aethoria?

The answers would have to wait. For now, there was a battle to be won. And with new allies joining the fight, the tide was about to turn.

Lyra raised the Crown of Whispers, its magic responding to her surge of determination. Whatever came next, she was ready to face it.

The real battle for Aethoria's soul had just begun.

TWENTY-ONE
A SPARK OF LIFE

The aftermath of the battle lay scattered across the plains outside the rebel stronghold. Lyra picked her way through the rubble, the Crown of Whispers a comforting weight on her forehead. Her father's unexpected return had turned the tide, sending Calidus and his forces into a chaotic retreat.

"Your Majesty!" Mira's voice cut through the haze of Lyra's thoughts. The young mage hurried toward her, her face flushed with excitement. "King Aldric asks for you. He's in the command tent."

Lyra nodded, her stomach churning with a mixture of anticipation and fear. What would she say to the father she had thought dead for so long?

As she approached the tent, voices drifted out - her father's deep timbre and Darius' measured tones. She paused to listen.

"I cannot trust her judgment," Aldric said. "She's too young, too inexperienced."

"With all due respect, Your Majesty," Darius countered, "Lyra has led us through impossible odds. Her people believe in her."

Lyra's heart swelled at Darius' defense. She squared her shoulders and pushed into the tent.

The conversation stopped as all eyes turned to her. Aldric stood tall and regal, his beard streaked with gray, but his eyes as piercing as she remembered. Darius stood beside him, tension evident in the set of his jaw.

"Father," Lyra said, her voice calmer than she felt.

Aldric's expression softened. "Lyra. My, how you've grown."

An uncomfortable silence stretched between them. There was so much to say, so many questions to ask, but where to begin?

Aren cleared his throat. "Maybe we should discuss our next move. Calidus won't stay quiet for long."

Grateful for the distraction, Lyra moved to the map-covered table in the center of the tent. As she leaned in to study their positions, a wave of dizziness washed over her. The room tilted alarmingly.

"Lyra?" Darius' worried voice seemed to come from far away.

She tried to answer, but darkness filled the edges of her vision. The last thing she saw was Darius lunging to catch her as she fell.

Lyra awoke to the familiar scent of healing herbs. She blinked, taking in the worried faces surrounding her cot - Darius, Mira, and her father.

"What happened?" she croaked, pulling herself to her feet.

Mira held a cup of water in her hands. "You fainted, Your Majesty. Probably exhaustion from the battle."

But there was something in the young mage's eyes, a mixture of awe and fear, that made Lyra pause.

"What aren't you telling me?"

Mira exchanged a look with Darius before speaking. "When I examined you, I felt... something. A spark of magic I've never encountered before. It's as if..."

"As if a new life is growing within you," Aldric finished, his voice grave.

The words hit Lyra like a physical blow. She looked at Darius and saw the shock and dawning realization on his face.

"I'm... pregnant?" The word felt foreign on her tongue.

Mira nodded. "It's still early, but yes. And the magical signature is unlike anything I've ever seen. It's as if the child's power is already manifesting."

Lyra's mind reeled. A child. Her child. Hers and Darius'. The implications washed over her in waves.

"The prophecy," Darius breathed. "A child born of royal and mage bloodlines..."

Aldric's eyes narrowed. "What prophecy?"

Before anyone could answer, the tent flap burst open. Aren stumbled in, his face pale. "Your Majesties, we have a problem. A messenger from the Vanguard has just arrived. Calidus..." He swallowed hard. "Calidus says he knows about the child. He demands we hand over Lyra and the baby or he'll raze every village in Aethoria to the ground."

The tent erupted into chaos. Voices clashed, arguing strategy and consequences. But Lyra heard none of it. Her hand went to her belly, still flat beneath her tunic. A life was growing there, a spark of magic and hope and terrifying potential.

"Enough!" Aldric's voice cut through the noise. "Everyone out. I need to speak to my daughter alone."

As the others filed out, Darius caught Lyra's eye. The love and fear she saw there mirrored her own tumultuous emotions. Then he was gone, leaving Lyra alone with the father she barely knew.

Aldric's stern facade crumbled as soon as they were alone. He went to Lyra's side and took her hand in his.

"Oh, my girl," he said softly. "I am so sorry. I never meant to put this burden on you."

Lyra blinked back tears. "Where have you been? All these years we thought you were dead."

Aldric sighed heavily. "It's a long story, and we don't have time for it now. But know this - everything I did was to protect you and Aethoria."

"And now?" Lyra asked. "What do we do now?"

Her father's eyes hardened. "Now we fight. Calidus cannot be allowed to get his hands on your child. The power he could wield... it would mean the end of everything we've fought for."

Lyra nodded, a plan already forming in her mind. "We must go on the offensive. Take the fight to him before he can gather his forces."

"It's too dangerous," Aldric protested. "In your condition-"

"In my condition, I am more powerful than ever," Lyra cut him off. She stood, the Crown of Whispers gleaming on her forehead. "This child is part of me, Father. His magic and mine are one. Together, we may be strong enough to end this war once and for all."

Aldric studied her face for a long moment before nodding slowly. "You have truly become a queen," he said, pride evident in his voice. "Very well. We'll follow your lead."

As they left the tent, Lyra's resolve hardened. She would fight not just for herself now, not just for her people, but for the future that was growing within her. A future that Calidus would stop at nothing to control.

Darius waited outside, worry etched into his features. Lyra took his hand, guiding it to rest on her belly.

"We're going to be parents," she said quietly.

His eyes widened, a mixture of joy and fear crossing his face. "Lyra, I... Are you sure about this? About fighting in your condition?"

She nodded, her voice calm. "I've never been more certain of anything. This child, our child, is the key to everything. We must protect it, no matter what the cost."

Darius pulled her close, his arms strong around her. "Then we will face this together. Whatever comes next."

As the rebels gathered, ready to hear their queen's orders, Lyra felt the weight of destiny settle on her shoulders. The Crown of Whispers hummed with power, responding to the new life within her.

She raised her voice, letting it carry over the assembled forces. "My friends, my people. The time has come to reclaim our kingdom. Calidus thinks he can use our love against us, threaten our families to make us submit. But he's wrong. Our love, our bonds, make us stronger."

A cheer rose from the crowd. Lyra continued, her voice growing stronger with each word.

"We will march on the capital at dawn. Not as rebels, but as true defenders of Aethoria. And we will not rest until our country is free!"

The roar of approval shook the ground. As the preparations began in earnest, Lyra turned to the horizon. Somewhere out there, Calidus waited, gloating over what he thought was his final victory.

But he had no idea what was in store for him.

A queen, a mage, and the most powerful child Aethoria had ever known.

The final battle for the soul of the kingdom was about to begin.

And Lyra would stop at nothing to ensure her child had a future worth fighting for.

TWENTY-TWO
RACE AGAINST TIME

The rebel army snaked through the Whispering Grove, a river of determination flowing toward the capital. Lyra rode at its head, the Crown of Whispers glittering in the dappled sunlight. Darius and Aren flanked her, their eyes constantly scanning for threats.

"How much further?" Lyra asked, one hand resting on her still-flat stomach.

Aren consulted a weathered map. "We should reach the outskirts of the city by nightfall. Assuming we don't run into any-"

A horn blast cut through the air, sharp and urgent. Lyra's head snapped up, her heart racing.

"Vanguard patrol!" The call echoed down the line.

In an instant, the orderly procession dissolved into chaos. Rebels grabbed for weapons, parents clutched their children.

Darius' hand found Lyra's arm. "We have to get you to safety."

She shook her head, magic already crackling at her fingertips. "I won't leave our people."

"Lyra," Darius' voice was deep, intense. "Think of the child. If anything happens to you-"

"Nothing will happen," she cut him off. "The baby is as much a part of this fight as I am."

Before he could argue further, the first Vanguard soldiers burst from the tree line. Arrows whistled through the air, met by a hail of rebel magic.

Lyra raised her hands and called upon the power of the crown. A shimmering barrier sprang into being, enveloping the rebel forces. Vanguard spells splashed harmlessly against it, but Lyra gasped at the drain on her energy.

"We can't stay here," Aren shouted over the din of battle. "We're too exposed!"

Lyra nodded grimly. "Fall back to the ravine. We'll make our stand there."

As the rebels retreated, Lyra held the shield. Sweat beaded on her brow, her vision blurred by the effort. The child inside her stirred, its budding magic intertwining with her own in ways she didn't yet understand.

They reached the ravine - a deep gash in the earth, its walls steep and treacherous. Lyra let the barrier fall, sagging in her saddle.

Darius was at her side in an instant. "Lyra? Are you all right?"

She managed a weak nod. "I'm fine. Just... tired."

His eyes narrowed, unconvinced, but there was no time to argue. The vanguard forces had regrouped, advancing on their position with grim purpose.

King Aldric's voice rose above the chaos. "Archers, to the high ground! Mages, prepare defensive spells. We will hold this line, no matter what the cost!"

Lyra straightened, drawing on reserves of strength she didn't know she possessed. The Crown of Whispers hummed, resonating with the magic of the land itself.

As the first wave of Vanguard soldiers charged, Lyra reached out. The earth itself answered her call. Roots erupted from the ground, ensnaring the attackers. Rocks torn from the canyon walls rained down upon them.

For a moment, it seemed they might hold. Then a familiar, chilling voice cut through the din of battle.

"I must say, I am impressed." Archmage Calidus materialized before them, dark magic swirling around him like a cloak. "You've led me on quite a chase, little queen."

Lyra's blood ran cold. She'd hoped for more time, more distance between them and the capital. But Calidus had found her, and now...

"Stand down, Calidus," King Aldric stepped forward, his sword gleaming. "You have lost. Accept it with what little dignity you have left."

Calidus laughed, the sound devoid of humor. "Lost? Oh, my old friend. I've already won." His gaze fell on Lyra, hunger in his eyes. "This child she carries... it's the key to everything. And you've brought it straight to me."

Lyra's hand went protectively to her belly. "You will never touch this child," she growled.

"Won't I?" Calidus raised an eyebrow. With a gesture, the air around them shimmered. Ghostly images appeared - villages, towns, cities across Aethoria. In each of them, Vanguard forces stood ready. "Surrender yourself and the child or watch your kingdom burn."

Horror washed over Lyra as she realized the extent of Calidus' threat. He'd positioned forces throughout Aethoria, ready to slaughter innocents at his command.

"You're bluffing," Aren growled, but doubt crept into his voice.

Calidus' smile was cold. "Am I? Are you willing to take that risk, Your Majesty? How many lives is your child worth?"

Time seemed to slow down as Lyra weighed her options. She could feel the eyes of her people upon her, waiting for her decision. The fate of Aethoria hung in the balance.

"I..." she began, but Darius cut her off.

"Take me instead," he said, stepping forward.

Lyra's heart clenched. "Darius, no!"

But he pressed on, his voice calm. "You want power, Calidus? I'm one of the most powerful mages in Aethoria. Let Lyra and the child go, and I'm yours."

Calidus considered for a moment, intrigue flickering in his eyes. "An interesting offer. But not quite what I'm looking for."

"Then take both of us," Darius countered. "Lyra and me. Think of the magical potential you could harness."

Lyra grabbed his arm, panic rising in her throat. "What are you doing?"

Darius met her gaze, his eyes filled with a mixture of love and determination. "Buying us time," he whispered. Then, louder, "So, Calidus? Do we have a deal?"

The Archmage stroked his chin, considering. "Very well. You and the queen will come with me. The child will remain here, under the protection of the oh-so-noble King Aldric."

"No!" Lyra's voice broke. "I will not leave my baby."

"You have no choice," Calidus sneered. "Unless you'd rather see your people suffer?"

The ghostly images flickered, screams of terror echoing from a dozen different places. Lyra's resolve crumbled.

"All right," she whispered. "You win."

A triumphant smile spread across Calidus' face. He raised his hands, dark magic gathering around them.

But before he could act, a blinding flash of blue light erupted from Lyra's midsection. She gasped and doubled over as waves of power radiated from her core.

"Lyra!" Darius caught her as she stumbled to her feet.

The world seemed to tip on its axis. Lyra's vision swam, filled with images she couldn't comprehend - a great tree whose roots stretched across Aethoria; a crown of starlight; a child with eyes that held the wisdom of ages.

When the light faded, Lyra found herself on her knees, cradled in Darius' arms. All around them, friend and foe alike stared in awe.

Calidus was the first to recover. "What trickery is this?" he demanded, his features distorted with rage.

Lyra struggled to her feet, new strength coursing through her veins. She could feel the child within her, its magic pulsing in time with her own heartbeat.

"No trickery," she said, her voice ringing with power. "This is the true magic of Aethoria. The magic you tried to control but never understood."

She raised her hands, and the Crown of Whispers came to life. The air around her shimmered with energy.

"You want this power so badly, Calidus?" Lyra's eyes flashed with defiance. "Then come and take it."

For a moment, no one moved. Then, with a roar of rage, Calidus lunged at Lyra. Dark magic crackled around him, a vortex of destructive power.

Lyra held her ground, the combined power of the crown and her unborn child surging through her. When Calidus' attack struck her magical barrier, the world erupted in a blast of light and sound.

When the dust settled, both Lyra and Calidus were gone.

Darius stared at the spot where they had stood, his heart pounding in his chest. "Lyra?" he shouted, his voice breaking. "LYRA!"

But there was no answer. Just the wind whistling through the gorge, carrying the faint echo of a baby's cry.

The battle for Aethoria's future had entered its final, desperate phase. And the outcome was anyone's guess.

TWENTY-THREE
THE ARCHMAGE'S OFFER

Lyra's eyes opened, her heart racing. She found herself in a vast chamber, its walls adorned with pulsing magical runes. The air hummed with power, making her skin tingle.

"Welcome to the heart of the Vanguard, Your Majesty." Calidus' voice echoed through the room. He stood across from her, a bemused smile playing on his lips. "I trust you find your accommodations... adequate?"

Lyra scrambled to her feet, a hand instinctively going to her stomach. The Crown of Whispers still sat on her forehead, its familiar weight oddly comforting.

"Where are we?" she demanded, her eyes searching for a way out.

Calidus spread his arms wide. "The Shattered Spire, of course. The heart of magical research in Aethoria. And soon to be the birthplace of a new era."

He took a step closer, his eyes shining with a disturbing mixture of hunger and admiration. "You have grown so strong, Lyra. Far beyond what I'd expected. That display in the ravine..." He shook his head, chuckling. "Magnificent."

Lyra's jaw clenched. "If you're planning to kill me, get on with it."

"Kill you?" Calidus looked genuinely shocked. "My dear girl, why would I destroy the very thing I've sought for so long?" He gestured to her midsection. "This child you are carrying... it is the key to everything. The perfect fusion of royal blood and raw magical potential."

A shiver ran down Lyra's spine. "You will never touch my baby," she snapped, magic crackling at her fingertips.

Calidus raised his hands in a soothing gesture. "You misunderstand me. I do not wish to harm your child. On the contrary, I wish to protect it. To nurture its potential. To create a world in which it can thrive."

He turned and waved a hand. The air shimmered, and suddenly they were surrounded by images of Aethoria. Cities gleaming with magical improvements. Crops growing in abundance. People living in peace and prosperity.

"This is the future I envision," Calidus said quietly. "A future where magic is not hoarded by the few, but shared for the benefit of all. Where your child can grow up without fear, without the burden of a divided kingdom."

Lyra's resolve wavered. The vision before her was... beautiful. Everything she'd ever wanted for Aethoria. But at what cost?

"And how many will die to achieve this 'utopia'?" she asked, her voice barely above a whisper.

Calidus sighed, the images fading. "Change always has a price, Lyra. You know that. But think of the lives that will be saved in the long run. The suffering that will be averted."

He stepped closer, his eyes boring into hers. "Join me. Let me teach you, guide you. Together, with the power of your child, we can remake Aethoria into something truly great."

Lyra's mind reeled. Part of her wanted to believe him, to imagine a world where her child could grow up safe and loved. But the memory of burning villages, of lives destroyed in Calidus' quest for power, held her back.

"And what of my people?" she asked. "The rebels who fought and died for freedom?"

Calidus waved his hand dismissively. "They will be pardoned, of course. Reintegrated into society. Their skills and dedication would be valuable in building our new world."

Lyra's eyes narrowed. "And Darius?"

A flicker of something - anger? jealousy? - crossed Calidus' face. "The traitor? He will face justice, of course. But I'm not unreasonable. If you would... intercede on his behalf, I'm sure we could come to some arrangement."

The implication hung heavy in the air. Lyra's life, her child's future, Darius' fate... all balanced on the edge of a knife.

Before she could answer, a tremor shook the chamber. Calidus frowned and turned to a shimmering magical display.

"Impossible," he muttered. "They couldn't have broken through our defenses that quickly."

Another shudder, stronger this time. The runes on the walls flickered.

Lyra's heart leapt. Could it be...?

Calidus turned to face her, his composure shattered. "This is your last chance, Lyra. Join me willingly, or I will be forced to take more... drastic measures."

As if in response to his threat, the Crown of Whispers came to life. Lyra gasped as the power surged through her, stronger than ever. She could feel her child's magic intertwining with her own, creating something entirely new.

"No," she said, her voice ringing with newfound strength. "I will never join you, Calidus. And you will never touch my child."

Fury distorted the Archmage's features. "So be it," he growled, dark magic coalescing around his hands. "I had hoped to do this the easy way, but you leave me no choice."

He thrust out his arms, unleashing a torrent of destructive energy. Lyra instinctively raised her hands, the magic of the crown forming a shimmering barrier.

The two forces collided with earth-shattering force. Lyra staggered back, her arms shaking with the effort of holding the shield. Calidus pressed his advantage, pouring more power into his attack.

"You cannot win this, girl," he growled. "The combined magic of the entire Vanguard flows through me. What hope do you have?"

Lyra gritted her teeth, feeling her defenses begin to crack. He was right - she was no match for his raw power. Not alone.

But she wasn't alone.

She closed her eyes and reached deep inside. To the spark of life growing in her womb. To the ancient magic of Aethoria that flowed through her veins.

"I am Lyra Valenwood," she whispered, her voice growing stronger with each word. "Rightful Queen of Aethoria. Protector of her people. And mother of its future."

The Crown of Whispers glowed with blinding light. Lyra felt her feet leave the ground as pure, untamed magic exploded from her core.

Calidus' eyes widened in shock and fear. "No," he breathed. "It's not possible..."

His words were cut off as Lyra's power slammed into him. The very air seemed to ripple and tear, reality itself bending under the strain.

For a moment, everything went white.

When Lyra's vision cleared, she found herself back on solid ground. The chamber lay in ruins around her, magical runes sputtering and dying on the cracked walls.

And there, sprawled in the rubble, lay Calidus. His once immaculate robes were torn and singed, his face pale with shock and exhaustion.

Lyra approached him cautiously, magic still crackling at her fingertips. "It's over, Calidus," she said quietly. "Surrender and I promise you will be treated fairly."

The Archmage looked up at her, a mixture of fear and awe in his eyes. "What are you?" he whispered.

Before Lyra could answer, the chamber doors burst open. Darius rushed in, sword drawn, followed closely by Aren and a group of rebels.

"Lyra!" Darius shouted, relief evident in his voice. He moved to her side, his eyes searching for any sign of injury. "Are you all right? The baby-"

"We're fine," Lyra assured him, a tired smile tugging at her lips. "Both of us."

Aren approached Calidus, binding the defeated Archmage's hands with magic-dampening restraints. "It's done, then?" he asked, looking to Lyra for confirmation.

She nodded, the weight of the moment settling on her shoulders. "It's done. The Vanguard is finished."

As the rebels secured the chamber and began to escort Calidus away, Lyra turned to Darius. She opened her mouth to speak, but she was suddenly overcome by exhaustion. Her knees buckled.

Darius caught her and held her gently. "I've got you," he murmured. "Rest now. You've done enough."

Lyra wanted to argue, to insist there was more to be done. But the steady beat of Darius' heart against her ear was too comforting to resist.

As her eyes closed, she caught a glimpse of something through a shattered window. A bright star, shining even in the daylight. A beacon of hope for the future of Aethoria.

Her future. Her future.

The war was over. But the real work of rebuilding her kingdom had only just begun.

And Lyra would face it as she had faced everything else - with courage, with love, and with the knowledge that she was never truly alone.

For in her heart, and in the child growing within her, the magic of Aethoria lived on.

Stronger than ever.

TWENTY-FOUR
RESCUE AND SACRIFICE

Darius crouched in the shadow of the Shattered Spire, his heart pounding. The imposing structure loomed over him, its twisted architecture a testament to the tainted magic of the Vanguard. Somewhere within those walls, Lyra waited - and with her, the fate of Aethoria.

"Are you sure about this?" Aren's whisper broke the tense silence. "It could be a trap."

Darius' jaw clenched. "It doesn't matter. We'll get her out."

Mira, her young face set with determination, nodded in agreement. "The stations are weakest here," she said, pointing to a section of the wall. "If we're going to break through, this is our best chance."

Darius took a deep breath and centered himself. The plan was risky, bordering on suicidal. But with Lyra and her unborn child in Calidus' grasp, they had no choice.

"Remember," he said to the small team of rebels, "our priority is Lyra. Once we have her, we leave. No heroics, no unnecessary risks."

A chorus of nods answered him. Darius raised his hands, feeling the magic rise within him. It was time.

With a gesture, he unleashed a torrent of energy at the wall. The stations flared to life, resisting his attack. Darius gritted his teeth and pressed harder. Sweat beaded his brow as he poured everything he had into the attack.

For a moment, nothing happened. Then, with a sound like shattering glass, the station collapsed.

"Now!" Darius shouted.

The rebels rushed forward, Aren leading the charge. They breached the outer defenses before the Vanguard guards could react.

Alarms blared as they fought their way deeper into the spire. Darius moved on autopilot, years of training taking over. His magic lashed out, incapacitating Vanguard soldiers left and right.

"This way!" Mira shouted, her magical senses guiding her through the labyrinthine corridors.

They rounded a corner and came face to face with a squad of elite Vanguard mages. Spells flew, the air crackling with arcane energy.

Darius deflected a bolt of lightning and retaliated with a wave of power that sent two mages flying. Aren's sword flashed, cutting through magical barriers as if they were paper.

But they were outnumbered, and Darius could see his team beginning to falter. Exhaustion and injuries were taking their toll.

"Fall back!" he ordered, creating a shield to cover their retreat. "Mira, find us another route!"

The young mage nodded, her eyes unfocused as she reached out with her magical senses. "There's a service tunnel two levels down," she said after a moment. "It should lead us to the central chambers."

They fought their way to a narrow stairwell and descended deeper into the bowels of the spire. The sounds of pursuit echoed behind them, growing closer with each passing second.

As they emerged into a dimly lit corridor, Darius felt a sudden, sharp pain in his side. He looked down to see a shard of magical energy protruding from his ribs.

"Darius!" Aren's voice seemed to come from far away. "You're hit!"

Darius waved him off, gritting his teeth against the pain. "It's nothing. Keep moving."

They pressed on, the service tunnel stretching endlessly before them. Darius felt his strength ebbing, each step harder than the last. But the thought of Lyra, their child, kept him going.

Finally they reached a heavy stone door. Mira placed her hand on it, her brow furrowed in concentration.

"She's close," she whispered. "I can feel her magic. But... there's something else. Something powerful."

Darius nodded grimly. "Calidus. Everyone, be prepared for anything."

With a combined effort, they forced the door open. The scene that greeted them stole the breath from Darius' lungs.

Lyra stood in the center of a vast chamber, bathed in blinding blue light. The Crown of Whispers blazed on her forehead, its power intertwined with the magic emanating from her unborn child. And before her, driven to his knees, stood Archmage Calidus.

"Impossible," the Archmage gasped, his face a mask of awe and terror.

Lyra's eyes found Darius, recognition and relief flooding her features. "Darius," she breathed.

The moment shattered as Calidus, seizing on the distraction, struck with a burst of dark magic. Lyra stumbled, her concentration shattered.

"No!" Darius roared. He lunged forward, ignoring the searing pain in his side.

Time seemed to slow. Darius saw Calidus gather his strength for a killing blow. He saw the fear in Lyra's eyes, her hands moving to protect her stomach. And he saw the path he must take.

Without hesitation, Darius threw himself between Lyra and Calidus. The Archmage's spell hit him square in the chest, knocking him off his feet and sending him crashing into the far wall.

Pain exploded through every nerve in his body. Darius heard Lyra scream, felt the surge of her magic as she fought back against Calidus. But it all seemed far away, unimportant.

As darkness crept in at the edges of his vision, Darius focused on Lyra's face. On the life growing inside her. Her child. Their future.

"I love you," he tried to say, but no sound came out.

The world faded to black.

Darius floated in a sea of nothing. No pain, no fear, no sense of time passing. Was this death?

A voice cut through the emptiness. Familiar, beloved.

"Darius. Darius, please. Come back to me."

Lyra?

He fought against the sound, against the comforting embrace of oblivion. Sensation slowly returned - the feel of a hand clasping his, the scent of healing herbs, the taste of copper in his mouth.

Darius opened his eyes.

Lyra's tear-stained face swam into focus above him. The Crown of Whispers still sat on her forehead, its glow muted but steady.

"There you are," she whispered, a watery smile spreading across her face. "I thought I'd lost you."

Darius tried to speak, but his throat was too dry. Lyra pressed a cup of water to his lips, supporting his head as he drank.

"What... happened?" he managed to croak.

"You saved me," Lyra said simply. "You saved us both." Her free hand went to her stomach, where the slightest hint of a lump was visible. "And then I... well, I'm not quite sure what I did. But Calidus is gone. The Vanguard fell."

Darius' eyes widened. "Gone? You mean..."

Lyra shook her head. "Not dead. But... contained. Stripped of his magic. He'll never hurt anyone again."

Relief washed over Darius, quickly followed by concern. "The others? Aren, Mira..."

"All safe," Lyra assured him. "Thanks to you."

Darius relaxed back onto the bed, wincing as the pain in his chest flared. "So it's over? We won?"

Lyra's expression became thoughtful. "The war is over, yes. But the real work is just beginning. Rebuilding Aethoria, healing the wounds left by the Vanguard... it won't be easy."

"Nothing worth doing ever is," Darius said, squeezing her hand.

A comfortable silence fell between them, broken only by the distant sounds of celebration drifting in from outside.

"Darius," Lyra said after a moment, her voice soft but intense. "What you did... throwing yourself in front of Calidus' spell... You could have died."

He met her gaze steadily. "I would do it again in a heartbeat."

Lyra's eyes flickered with unshed tears. "I know. That's what scares me." She took a deep breath. "I can't lose you. Not now, not ever. This child, our child... they'll need both of us."

Darius' heart swelled. He reached up and cupped Lyra's cheek. "I'm not going anywhere. Whatever comes next, we'll face it together. I promise."

Lyra leaned into his touch, a smile playing on her lips. "Together," she agreed.

As if in response to her words, a warm glow emanated from Lyra's midsection. The Crown of Whispers pulsed in harmony, its magic intertwined with that of her unborn child.

Darius gasped as he felt a tendril of that power reach out to him, soothing his injuries, knitting flesh and bone.

"I think," Lyra said, wonder in her voice, "our little one agrees."

Darius laughed, ignoring the pain in his ribs. For the first time in what felt like ages, hope blossomed in his chest - bright and unshakable.

The road ahead would be long and full of challenges. But with Lyra by his side, their child growing strong within her, Darius knew they could face anything.

The future of Aethoria was theirs to forge. And they would make it a future worth fighting for.

As the sounds of celebration grew louder outside, Darius pulled Lyra close and captured her lips in a kiss that held all the promise of tomorrow.

Whatever came next, they would face it together.

As a family.

TWENTY-FIVE
A KINGDOM OF SHADOWS

Dawn crept over the walls of the restored palace, painting shadows across a city Lyra barely recognized. Where Vanguard towers had once dominated the skyline, wild magic had sculpted new forms: crystalline spires that caught the light like prisms, living architecture that breathed with the pulse of the land. These forms were beautiful but unsettling, a constant reminder that nothing could go back to how it was.

She stood at the council chamber windows, watching workers rebuild what the war had broken. Former rebels worked alongside reformed Vanguard soldiers, their old uniforms replaced by the blue and silver of the new unified guard. On the surface, it's a picture of cooperation. But Lyra saw the tensions in rigid shoulders and careful distances kept.

"The delegation from the Western Provinces is refusing to attend today's meeting," Aren reported from behind her. His new formal attire still sat uncomfortably on his warrior's frame. "They say they won't negotiate with 'Vanguard sympathizers.'"

Lyra's fingers traced the Crown of Whispers, its power a steady thrum against her temples. "And what of the former Vanguard territories?"

"Lord Garrick reports growing unrest. The common people fear wild magic more than they ever feared the Vanguard. At least the old ways were predictable."

"Predictable but dead." Lyra turned from the window. The council chamber was filling with her advisors - faces that had once been enemies, now bound together by necessity and fragile trust. "The old ways nearly destroyed Aethoria. We can't go back."

"No one wants to go back," Darius said quietly from his place at the table. His presence still drew wary looks from some of the older council members, but none could deny his value as an advisor. Or his place at Lyra's side. "But people need stability. Structure. Right now, we're giving them chaos."

He gestured to the maps spread across the table. Red marks showed where wild magic had transformed the landscape - forests springing up overnight, rivers changing course, mountains reshaping themselves. Blue marks showed the refugee camps, swelling with displaced people who could no longer live in their ancestral homes.

"The Keepers are doing what they can," Mira offered. The young mage had grown into her role as head of the new magical order, though shadows of exhaustion marked her eyes. "But we can only guide the wild magic, not control it. That's the whole point."

"The point," Lord Carrick growled, "is that people are suffering. Winter's coming, and half our farmland has been transformed into crystal forests. Beautiful, yes, but you can't eat beauty."

Murmurs of agreement rippled through the chamber. Lyra felt the weight of their expectations, their fears. The crown grew heavier on her brow.

"What do you suggest?" she asked, making eye contact with each council member. "Should we try to suppress the wild magic? Lock it away as the Vanguard did? We all saw how well that worked."

"Of course not," Lady Elara spoke up. The merchant princess had been one of the first to pledge support to the new regime, recognizing which way the winds were blowing. "But perhaps we could... direct it. Channel it towards useful purposes."

"You mean to control it," Darius said flatly.

"I mean survive!" Lady Elara shot back. "What good is magical purity if we all starve?"

The argument that followed was one Lyra had heard a dozen times before. The practical need for rebuilding versus the philosophical imperative to respect wild magic's nature. The demands of the common people versus the warnings of the Keepers. The desire for quick solutions versus the need for sustainable change.

She let them argue, watching the alliances and resentments play out across the table. This was the real work of rebuilding —not just stone and timber, but trust, understanding, and compromise.

A flicker of movement caught her eye. One of the crystal formations outside the window was growing, its faceted surface catching the morning sun. It was beautiful and terrible, like so much of what they'd unleashed.

"Enough," she said quietly. The word carried weight, silencing the council chamber. "We all want the same thing - a stable, prosperous Aethoria. But we won't get there by falling back into old patterns of control and dominance."

She stood, letting her power fill the room - not as a threat, but as a reminder. "The wild magic is part of us now. Part of our land, our people, our future. We must learn to live with it, not fight it."

"And how do we do that?" someone asked. "Practically speaking?"

Lyra smiled. This was the opening she'd been waiting for. "I have a proposal. One that will require cooperation from all of you."

She outlined her plan: a network of Keeper stations throughout the kingdom, working with local communities to understand and guide the wild magic in their regions, and training for those with magical sensitivity. New trade routes accounting for the changed landscape; and, most importantly, a council system that would give voice to all peoples of Aethoria, from noble to commoner, mage to merchant.

"It won't be easy," she concluded. "It will require all of us to change how we think about power, about control, about leadership itself. But I believe it's our best chance to build something truly new. Something worthy of everything we sacrificed to get here."

The silence that followed was thoughtful rather than hostile. She could see them considering, calculating, wondering if they could trust each other enough to make it work.

Finally, Lord Garrick spoke. "It's ambitious. Perhaps impossible." He smiled grimly. "Then again, they said the same about defeating the Vanguard."

One by one, the council members nodded. Not in wholehearted agreement - there would be arguments about details, compromises to negotiate, trust to build. But it was a start.

As the meeting adjourned, Darius lingered behind. "You know this won't solve everything," he said softly. "There are still those who resist any change, who'd rather see us fail than admit the old ways were wrong."

"I know." Lyra's hand found his, drawing strength from his touch. "But we didn't fight for easy answers. We fought for the chance to find our own way forward."

She looked out at her changed city, at the crystal spires catching the morning light. Not beautiful or terrible, she realized, but both at once, like all great changes, like growth itself.

"Besides," she said, managing a smile, "when have we ever taken the easy path?"

Darius's laugh was warm against her ear. But before he could respond, a guard burst into the chamber, face pale with urgency.

"Your Majesty! Reports from the border - something's coming. Something impossible."

Lyra exchanged a look with Darius. Of course. Peace was never guaranteed. Only the chance to fight for it.

"Gather the council," she commanded. "And send word to the Keepers."

The real work was just beginning.

TWENTY-SIX
TRUST DIVIDED

The war room hummed with tension as Lyra studied the reports spread across the tactical table. Crystal markers showed the progression of... whatever was coming across their borders. Not an army - at least, not one that moved in any way she recognized. But the devastation it left in its wake was undeniable.

"Three villages empty," Aren reported, moving another marker into place. "No signs of violence. No bodies. They just... vanished. Along with every trace of wild magic in the area."

"Like it was never there," Mira added. The young Keeper's face was drawn with exhaustion from attempts to scry the affected regions. "The ley lines are silent. Dead."

A chill ran down Lyra's spine. Since the fall of the Vanguard, wild magic had become woven into the very fabric of their society. Villages adapted to its presence and learned to work with its strange gifts and occasional chaos. To have it suddenly absent...

"What do the survivors say?" Darius asked. He stood at Lyra's side, close enough that she could draw strength from his presence without appearing to lean on him. They'd learned that balance - support without weakness, love without vulnerability, at least in public.

Lord Garrick cleared his throat. "Those who escaped in time speak of shadows. Movements glimpsed from the corner of the eye. A feeling of... wrongness. Then nothing."

"Shadows," Lady Elara scoffed, but Lyra noted the tremor in her voice. "We need facts, not ghost stories. My trading caravans can't operate if-"

A commotion at the door cut her off. A messenger burst in, face pale with urgency. "Your Majesty! The Western Delegation - they're gone!"

"Gone?" Lyra's fingers tightened on the edge of the table. "What do you mean, gone?"

"Their entire camp, the one they set up rather than stay in the palace..." The messenger swallowed hard. "It's empty. Just like the villages."

Silence fell over the war room. The Western Delegation had been vocal opponents of Lyra's reforms, but they represented a significant portion of Aethoria's population. Their disappearance wouldn't just create political chaos - it would shatter the fragile trust they'd been building.

"It's happening here," Mira whispered. "In the capital itself."

As if in response to her words, the crystals that had grown throughout the city since wild magic's awakening began to dim. Their usual luminescence faded, leaving them looking more like glass than living stone.

"We have to evacuate," Aren said, already moving toward the door. "Get our people somewhere defensible-"

"Where?" Darius's question cut through the rising panic. "If this thing can reach us here, in the heart of our power, where could we possibly hide?"

"We don't hide." Lyra's quiet voice reached every corner of the room. "We fight."

Lady Elara laughed, a brittle sound. "Fight what? Shadows? Empty villages? How do you propose we battle an enemy we can't even see?"

"By seeing it." Lyra straightened, letting her connection to the Crown of Whispers flow through her. Its power felt different now - not the raw force it had been during the war, but something more profound. More attuned to the fabric of reality itself. "Mira, gather the Keepers, all of them. Aren, I want every warrior who can sense magic, no matter how slightly. Lord Garrick..."

"Your Majesty?"

"You said once that the Vanguard had ways of tracking magical disturbances. Methods they kept secret from the rest of us."

The former Vanguard commander's mechanical arm whirred as he shifted uncomfortably. "Forbidden techniques. Dangerous ones."

"More dangerous than what's happening now?"

Garrick met her gaze for a long moment before nodding slowly. "I'll gather what we need."

"Your Majesty," Lady Elara stepped forward, her merchant's pragmatism warring with genuine concern. "Even if we can see this threat, how can we be sure it's something we can fight? Perhaps it would be better to negotiate. Find out what it wants."

"It wants what it's already taking," Darius said grimly. "Our magic. Our life. Our very essence."

"Then why?" Someone asked from the back of the room. "Why now? Why us?"

Lyra looked out the window at her changed city. At the crystal spires going dark one by one. At the wild magic that had reshaped their world for better or worse.

"Because we dared to change," she said softly. "Because we chose a different path than the one laid out for us. And something... something out there couldn't allow that."

She turned back to her council, seeing the fear in their eyes and also their determination. They hadn't come this far, hadn't sacrificed so much to give up now.

"Prepare yourselves," she commanded. "In one hour, we-"

A scream cut through the air - high, terrible, and abruptly silenced. Then another. And another.

Lyra raced to the window. Horror froze her breath in her lungs.

Shadows moved through the streets below. Not natural shadows, but something darker. Deeper. They flowed like liquid night, consuming everything they touched. Where they passed, the wild magic died. Colors faded. Life itself seemed to... stop.

And they were heading for the palace.

"Seal the doors!" Aren shouted, already organizing a defense. "Get everyone inside!"

But Lyra saw the truth in the way the shadows moved. In their inexorable advance.

No door would hold them. No wall would stop them. They were coming.

And she had a terrible feeling she knew why.

"Darius," she said quietly, taking his hand. "If something happens..."

He squeezed her fingers, understanding in his eyes. "Together," he promised. "Whatever comes."

She nodded, then turned to face her council. It's time for one last stand.

One last chance to prove that what they'd built was worth fighting for.

It's worth dying for, if necessary.

The shadows reached the palace steps.

And Lyra Valenwood, Queen of Aethoria, prepared to face the darkness that came to unmake her world.

TWENTY-SEVEN
POWER OF UNITY

Raw power blazed from the Crown of Whispers as Lyra faced the advancing shadows. The war room had become their last bastion, its walls reinforced with every protection the Keepers could muster. Around her, former enemies stood united - Vanguard and rebel, noble and commoner, all that remained of Aethoria's leadership.

"The wards won't hold much longer," Mira reported, sweat beading her brow as she maintained the magical barriers. Through the windows, they could see the shadows flowing up the palace walls like liquid darkness, consuming everything they touched. Where they passed, even the memory of magic seemed to fade.

"Lord Garrick?" Lyra's voice remained steady despite the fear clawing at her chest. "Are you ready?"

The former Vanguard commander stood at the center of a complex array of crystals and runes - forbidden Vanguard technology merged with wild magic in ways that would have been unthinkable months ago. "Almost. But Your Majesty... this could kill you."

"If we do nothing, we're already dead." Lyra moved to the center of the array, feeling its power resonate with her own. "Everyone knows their part?"

Nods around the room. They'd had precious little time to prepare, but desperation bred efficiency. The Keepers formed a circle, channeling what remained of the wild magic through ancient ley lines. Former Vanguard mages stood ready with their precise, controlled power. And at the heart of it all, the Crown of Whispers pulsed with possibility.

A sound like shattering glass echoed through the palace. The outer wards were failing.

"Now!" Lyra commanded.

Garrick activated the array. Pain shot through Lyra's body as different forms of magic collided within her - wild and controlled, ancient and new, all seeking balance. The Crown of Whispers flared like a newborn star.

For a moment, she saw everything. The shadows were not just darkness but absence. Void. A hunger that consumed magic itself, leaving nothing but empty husks behind. And they served something vast, cold, and patient that saw their vibrant, chaotic world as an affront to proper order.

"Look!" Someone gasped.

Through the windows, they could see the shadows pause in their advance. The darkness roiled and twisted as if sensing a new presence. A worthy opponent.

Then, it surged forward with renewed force.

The inner wards shattered. Darkness poured into the war room like a flood. Mira screamed as her magical barriers dissolved. Aren's sword passed harmlessly through the shadows as they reached for him with tendrils of void.

"Hold the circle!" Lyra shouted. Power continued to build within her, threatening to tear her apart. "Whatever happens, hold-"

A shadow wrapped around her throat, cutting off her words. Cold, unlike anything she'd ever felt, seeped into her bones. She saw her own magic, her very life force, being drawn out into the darkness.

Then Darius was there, his hand finding hers. The touch sent energy surging through her - not just his power, but his warmth, his love, his absolute refusal to let her face this alone.

Other hands joined theirs. Mira, channeling the wild magic she'd learned to guide. Aren, lending the strength that had kept him fighting through countless battles. Lord Garrick, offering the precision and control he'd mastered over decades. Lady Elara, contributing the subtle power that flowed through merchant routes and trade agreements.

One by one, every person in the room joined the circle. Noble and commoner, mage and warrior, each offering their unique gifts to the whole.

The Crown of Whispers sang with power, unlike anything Lyra had ever felt. Not the raw force she'd wielded in battle or the wild magic that had reshaped their land. This was something new. Something born of unity rather than control, of harmony rather than dominance.

She opened herself fully to it, understanding at last what the crown had been trying to teach her all along.

True power did not come from strength, control, or even wild magic itself. It came from a connection. From the bonds between people who chose to stand together despite their differences, from the courage to face darkness not alone but as one.

Lyra raised her free hand, and pure light blazed from her palm. No destroying the shadows but illuminating them, revealing their true nature, and showing them that here, in this room, they would find no fear to feed on. There is no division to exploit, only unity.

The shadows recoiled. Their darkness began to dissipate, unable to maintain form in the face of such radiance.

But it wasn't enough. Through her enhanced sight, Lyra could see more shadows gathering. An endless tide of void, ready to consume everything they'd built.

"I have to go deeper," she gasped. "Have to reach the source-"

"No!" Darius's grip tightened. "It'll kill you!"

"If I don't, it'll kill everyone." She met his eyes, seeing her own pain reflected there. "You know I have to try."

Before he could argue further, she reached out with her enhanced senses, following the shadows back to their origin. Back to the vast, cold presence that had sent them.

FOOLISH CHILD, it spoke directly into her mind. *YOUR WORLD IS AN ABERRATION. WILD MAGIC WAS NEVER MEANT TO RUN FREE. WE WILL RESTORE PROPER ORDER.*

"Our world is not an aberration," Lyra replied, letting her voice carry the power of everyone connected to her. It's evolution, growth, and change."

CHANGE BRINGS CHAOS. CHAOS BRINGS DESTRUCTION.

"Change brings hope," Lyra countered. "The hope of something better. Something new."

She poured everything she had into one final surge of power, not attacking the presence but showing it the truth of her words. She showed Aethoria not as it had been or even as it was but as it could be—a world where different magics coexist in harmony, where former enemies worked together to build something greater than themselves, and where unity was found not in rigid control but in celebrating their differences.

THIS CANNOT BE ALLOWED, the presence insisted, but she sensed uncertainty in its cold voice.

"It already is," Lyra said softly. "Look."

She opened her awareness fully, letting the presence see through her eyes. She saw the people in this room standing together despite everything that should have torn them apart. She saw wild magic and controlled magic flowing together in perfect balance. She saw the Crown of Whispers not as a tool of power but as a symbol of connection.

For a moment that felt like an eternity, nothing happened.

Then, slowly, the shadows began to retreat not just from the war room but also from all of Aethoria. The void closed, taking its cold presence with it.

YOU HAVE CHOSEN A DIFFICULT PATH, it said as it faded. *IT MAY YET LEAD TO YOUR DESTRUCTION.*

"Maybe," Lyra acknowledged. "But it's our choice to make."

The presence vanished, and warmth and color flooded back into the world. The crystal spires blazed with renewed light, wild magic surging through them like blood returning to numbed limbs.

Lyra swayed on her feet as the power that had filled her receded. Multiple hands steadied her - Darius, Mira, Aren, and others. She looked around at their exhausted but triumphant faces, feeling the bonds that now connected them all.

"Is it over?" Lady Elara asked, her usual composure shaken.

"For now." Lyra managed a tired smile. "But it'll be back. Or something else will. There will always be forces that fear change, that seek to impose their version of order."

"And we'll face them the same way we faced this one," Darius said firmly. "Together."

Murmurs of agreement filled the room. Lyra felt hope bloom in her chest as she saw former enemies clasping hands, sharing water, and tending to each other's wounds. The shadows had tried to divide them but had only succeeded in forging stronger bonds.

She looked out the window at her changed city - not just changed by wild magic now, but by the choices they'd made. The paths they'd chosen. The trust they'd built.

The Crown of Whispers hummed softly, its power a reminder of everything they'd learned. Everything they'd become.

They had faced the darkness and emerged stronger.

Whatever came next, they would face it the same way.

Together.

As one.

TWENTY-EIGHT
THE FINAL DUEL

The air crackled with arcane energy as Lyra and Darius approached the Shattered Spire. Once a symbol of the Vanguard's oppression, the towering structure now pulsated with corrupted wild magic, its twisted form a blight on the Aethorian skyline.

"Are you sure about this?" Darius whispered, his hand gripping the hilt of his sword.

Lyra nodded, the Crown of Whispers humming on her forehead. "We end this today. For Aurora. For all of Aethoria."

They had left their daughter in the care of Mira and King Aldric, the pain of separation eased only by the knowledge of what was at stake. If they failed here, there would be no future for Aurora to inherit.

As they neared the base of the spire, a shimmer in the air caught Lyra's attention. She reached out a hand, and magic came to life. "Wait!"

Darius froze, his eyes scanning their surroundings. "What is it?"

"A station," Lyra murmured, her fingers tracing invisible patterns in the air. "Complex. Calidus has been busy."

She closed her eyes, reaching out with her magical senses. The crown amplified her power, allowing her to see the intricate web of spells surrounding the spire. With a twist of her wrist and a muttered incantation, she unraveled a section of the station.

"There," she said, opening her eyes. "We have a way in. But he'll know we're here now."

Darius nodded grimly. "Then we'd better hurry."

They slipped through the gap in the stations, the oppressive aura of corrupted magic increasing with each step. As they entered the Spire itself, Lyra's stomach churned. The once pristine halls were now warped and twisted, pulsing with sickly energy.

"This way," Darius said, pointing to a spiral staircase. "The heart of corruption will be at the top."

They ascended quickly, meeting no resistance. The silence was unnerving, broken only by their footsteps and the occasional groan of the building itself.

Finally, they reached the top chamber. The massive doors swung open at their approach, as if inviting them in.

"Welcome, Your Majesty," Calidus' voice rang out, dripping with mockery. "I have been expecting you."

The Archmage stood in the center of the room, surrounded by swirling sands of dark magic. He looked different - older, more haggard, but with a disturbing gleam in his eyes.

"It's over, Calidus," Lyra declared, magic crackling at her fingertips. "Surrender now and we will show you mercy."

Calidus laughed, the sound echoing unnaturally. "Mercy? Oh, my dear girl. You have no idea of the powers you are up against."

He raised his hands, and the swirls coalesced into a pulsing orb of energy. "Behold the true power of Aethoria! Wild magic, tamed and perfected!"

Lyra's eyes widened as she recognized the corrupted essence within the orb. "The heart of Aethoria... What have you done?"

"I have unlocked its true potential," Calidus crowed. "No longer will magic be bound by petty morality or the whims of nature. With this power, I can reshape reality itself!"

Darius stepped forward, his sword glowing with magical energy. "You are mad, Calidus. This power was never meant to be controlled by one person."

"And who are you to decide?" Calidus sneered. "A traitor to the Vanguard, pretending to be a king?"

Lyra's anger flared. "Enough! We'll take you in, Calidus. One way or another."

She stretched out her hands, channeling the power of the crown. A wave of pure magical power surged toward Calidus. But the Archmage merely smiled, deflecting the attack with a casual gesture.

"Is this the best the Queen of Aethoria can muster?" he taunted.

Darius lunged, his enchanted blade singing through the air. Calidus parried with a summoned staff of dark energy, and the two weapons collided in a shower of sparks.

Lyra seized the opportunity, weaving a complex binding spell. Tendrils of blue light shot toward Calidus, attempting to ensnare him. But the corrupted magic surrounding him lashed out, shredding her spell before it could take hold.

"You'll have to do better than that," Calidus growled, sending Darius spinning back with a burst of power.

The battle raged on, magic and steel clashing in a deadly dance. But for every attack launched by Lyra and Darius, Calidus had a counter. The corrupted heart of Aethoria pulsed with every effort, feeding him with seemingly limitless power.

"We can't beat him like this," Darius panted, falling back to Lyra's side. "He's too strong."

Lyra's mind raced, searching for a solution. Then, in a moment of clarity, she understood.

"We don't have to beat him," she said quietly. "We need to free the heart."

Darius' eyes widened with understanding. He nodded, a silent plan passing between them.

They launched a coordinated attack, Darius driving Calidus back with a flurry of sword strikes while Lyra bombarded him with spells. The Archmage laughed, easily parrying their attacks.

"Is that all you have?" he taunted. "Pathetic!"

But in his arrogance, he failed to see Lyra's true goal. With Darius distracting Calidus, she focused her magic not on the Archmage, but on the corrupted heart floating behind him.

The Crown of Whispers blazed with power as Lyra reached out to the very essence of Aethoria. "Remember who you are," she whispered to the heart. "Remember the balance you were meant to maintain."

For a moment, nothing happened. Then, with a sound like shattering glass, cracks appeared in the dark shell surrounding the Heart.

Calidus spun around, his face contorted with rage and fear. "No! What are you doing?"

He lunged for the heart, but Darius intercepted him, and their weapons locked once more.

"Now, Lyra!" Darius shouted.

Lyra poured every ounce of her power into the spell, drawing strength from the crown, from her love for Darius and Aurora, from her connection to the land itself.

The corrupted vessel exploded outward. Pure, unbridled magic flooded the chamber. Lyra gasped as she felt the true essence of Aethoria wash over her - ancient, wild, and gloriously free.

Calidus screamed, the dark magic he'd wielded turning on him as the heart refused his control. His form began to warp and twist, consumed by the very power he'd tried to master.

"What have you done?" he wailed, his voice distorted. "I could have given you anything!"

Lyra stood tall, the Crown of Whispers shining like a star. "We never wanted your version of everything, Calidus. Aethoria deserves to be free."

With a final, anguished scream, Calidus dissolved into motes of light, absorbed back into the heart of Aethoria.

For a moment, there was silence. Then the Spire began to shake.

"We have to go," Darius urged, grabbing Lyra's hand. "The whole place is coming down!"

They raced down the spiral staircase as the Spire crumbled around them. Chunks of masonry rained down, narrowly missing them as they ran.

They burst out of the entrance just as the spire collapsed. A shockwave of pure magical energy exploded outward, washing over them and spreading across the land.

Lyra and Darius watched in awe as the corruption that had plagued Aethoria burned away. The wild magic, freed from Calidus' influence, settled into a new equilibrium. Nature and magic, once at odds, found harmony.

As the dust settled, Lyra turned to Darius. His face was streaked with dirt and blood, but his eyes shone with love and relief.

"We made it," she breathed, hardly believing it herself.

Darius pulled her close, his lips meeting hers in a kiss that held all the promise of tomorrow. "We did it," he murmured against her mouth. "It's over. We're free."

But even as they embraced, Lyra couldn't shake the feeling that this was only the beginning. The heart of Aethoria was free, yes, but with that freedom came new challenges, new responsibilities.

As if in response to her thoughts, the Crown of Whispers pulsed softly. Lyra's mind filled with visions of the future - a land in bloom, magic and nature in perfect balance, but also glimpses of darker possibilities.

She drew back to meet Darius's questioning gaze. "We have work to do," she said quietly.

He nodded, understanding in his eyes. "Together?"

Lyra smiled and took his hand. "Always."

As they made their way back to the capital, to their daughter and the future they'd fought so hard to secure, Lyra's heart swelled with hope and determination.

The final battle had been won. But the true challenge of building a new Aethoria was just beginning.

And she was ready to meet it head on.

TWENTY-NINE
A NEW DAWN

The throne room of Aethoria buzzed with nervous energy. Lyra stood before the ornate seat of power, the Crown of Whispers gleaming on her forehead. Darius stood at her side, his presence a calming force.

"Are you ready?" he whispered, his hand finding hers.

Lyra took a deep breath and squeezed his fingers. "As I'll ever be."

The great doors swung open and the assembled crowd fell silent. Nobles, merchants, former rebels, and even a few former Vanguard members filled the hall, their eyes fixed on their new queen.

King Aldric stepped forward, his voice ringing clear and strong. "People of Aethoria, I present to you Queen Lyra Valenwood, rightful heir to the throne and protector of our realm."

The crowd cheered, but Lyra could see the uncertainty in some faces. She raised her hand to silence them.

"My friends," she began, her voice carrying to every corner of the room. "We stand at the dawn of a new era for Aethoria. The war is over, Calidus is defeated, and wild magic is free once again."

Murmurs rippled through the gathering. Lyra continued.

"But our work is far from over. The scars of the conflict run deep, and the balance of magic in our land remains precarious. It is up to us to forge a new path forward - one of harmony, justice and shared prosperity."

She gestured to Darius. "With the guidance of those who have fought and sacrificed for our freedom, we will rebuild Aethoria stronger than ever."

A voice called out from the crowd - Lord Garrick, a former Vanguard commander. "And what of those who served the old regime? Will there be pardons?"

Lyra met his gaze. "There will be justice tempered with mercy. Those who truly seek redemption and wish to contribute to our new society will be given the opportunity to do so."

Another voice, this time Lady Elara of the Western Provinces. "Your Majesty, what of the wild magic? Reports from across the kingdom tell of unprecedented changes - forests growing overnight, new species appearing. How can we hope to control it?"

"We don't," Lyra replied firmly. "Wild magic is part of Aethoria itself. Our task is not to control it, but to understand it and learn to live in harmony with it."

She turned and gestured to a group standing off to the side. Mira stood at their head, cradling baby Aurora in her arms.

"To this end, I am creating the Order of the Whispered Crown. These mages and scholars will study the new magic, help our people adapt to the changes, and ensure that the balance we've fought so hard for is maintained."

Mira stepped forward and bowed her head. "We are honored to serve, Your Majesty."

A wave of excitement swept through the crowd. But not everyone was pleased.

Lord Barristen, an old nobleman from the eastern reaches, spoke up. "Fine words, Your Majesty. But how will you pay for all this? Our coffers are empty, our fields lie fallow. The common people are crying out for food and shelter, not magical research."

Lyra's jaw tightened, but before she could respond, Darius stepped forward.

"My lord, you raise a valid concern. But consider this - with wild magic properly understood and harnessed, we can regrow our crops in a fraction of the time. We can heal our sick and injured, reducing the strain on our resources. The work of the Order will benefit all of Aethoria, not just a select few."

Barristen grumbled, but others nodded in agreement. Lyra gave Darius a grateful look before addressing the crowd once more.

"We face many challenges, it's true. But we also have an unprecedented opportunity to reshape our kingdom for the better. I ask for your trust, your patience, and your support as we embark on this journey together."

She raised her voice, infusing it with all the determination she felt. "Together, there is nothing we cannot overcome. For Aethoria!"

The assembly echoed the call, their voices joining in a roar of hope and determination. "For Aethoria!"

As the cheers died down, Lyra prepared to dismiss the assembly. But a commotion at the back of the hall caught her attention.

A messenger burst through the doors, his face pale with urgency. He sprinted to the foot of the throne and dropped to one knee.

"Your Majesty," he gasped, out of breath. "News from the border. An army is approaching from the south - flying the banner of Shadowmere."

The room erupted in chaos. Shadowmere, Aethoria's longtime rival, had been quiet during the civil war. But now, with Aethoria weakened...

Lyra's mind raced. She locked eyes with Darius, seeing her own concern reflected there. Then she straightened, her voice cutting through the panicked chatter.

"Silence!"

The room fell silent, all eyes on their queen.

"How long before they reach our borders?" Lyra demanded.

The messenger swallowed hard. "Three days, Your Majesty. Perhaps four."

Lyra nodded, her expression grim. "Then we have work to do. Lord Garrick, mobilize what's left of our forces. Lady Elara, I need an inventory of our supplies and a plan for evacuating the border towns if necessary."

She turned to Mira. "Gather the order. We need to know if the wild magic can be used in our defense."

As the nobles and officials rushed to carry out her orders, Lyra felt a tug on her sleeve. She looked down to see Aurora, awake and alert in Mira's arms. The baby's eyes shimmered with an unearthly light, and for a moment Lyra saw a flash of... something. A vision of battles yet to come, of challenges that would test them all.

She blinked, and the moment passed. But the weight of what she'd seen settled heavily on her shoulders.

Darius appeared at her side, his face etched with concern. "Lyra? What is it?"

She met his gaze, her voice deep and urgent. "This is only the beginning. Shadowmere, the wild magic, the remnants of the Vanguard... We've won the war, but the real battle for Aethoria's future is just beginning."

Darius nodded, his hand finding hers. "Then we will face it together. As we always have."

Lyra squeezed his fingers, drawing strength from his unwavering support. She looked out over the bustling throne room, at the people who had placed their trust in her. At the daughter who represented their hopes for the future.

The road ahead was fraught with danger and uncertainty. But as the Crown of Whispers hummed with power, Lyra Valenwood - rebel, mage, queen, and mother - knew one thing for certain.

Whatever came next, she would meet it head on. For her people. For her family. For Aethoria.

The true test of her reign was about to begin.

THIRTY
THE NEXT CHAPTER

Dawn painted Aethoria's skies in shades of amber and rose, the first rays catching on the crystalline spires that had sprouted in the wake of the wild magic's awakening. From her balcony in the restored palace, Lyra watched shadows retreat from her city – a city that bore little resemblance to the one she'd first fought to save.

These days, the Crown of Whispers sat lighter on her brow, as if it, too, had evolved with the changing realm. Beside her, Darius cradled Aurora, their daughter's otherworldly eyes tracking the movements of invisible currents that only she could see.

"A messenger arrived from the southern provinces," Darius said softly, careful not to disturb Aurora's fascination with the magical eddies. "The shadow giants have been sighted again."

Lyra's hands tightened on the balcony's rail, weathered stone rough beneath her fingers. "How many?"

"Three. Larger than before." He shifted Aurora to one arm, his free hand finding the small of Lyra's back. "The border villages are evacuating, but—"

"But they shouldn't have to." The words came out sharper than she intended. A year of peace, of rebuilding, of learning to balance motherhood with monarchy – and now this. "Have the Keepers had any success understanding where they come from?"

"Mira thinks—" Darius began, but a knock at the chamber door interrupted him.

Aren entered, his captain's insignia catching the morning light. The past year had added silver to his temples but taken none of the steel from his spine. "Your Majesties. The war council awaits."

Lyra nodded, squaring her shoulders. In the early days of her reign, she'd practiced this moment in mirrors – the transformation from woman to queen. Now, it came as naturally as breathing. "Send word to the border settlements. Any who wish to seek shelter in the capital will find it."

"Already done, Your Majesty." A ghost of a smile touched Aren's lips. "I took the liberty."

"Of course you did." The familiar exchange eased some of the tension from her shoulders. These were her people now, all of them – not just subjects, but family forged in fire and magic.

They made their way to the war room, where maps and tactical displays covered every surface. The assembled council members rose at her entrance – former rebels and reformed Vanguard alike united under a crown that served rather than ruled.

"The situation," she said, taking her place at the head of the table. It wasn't a question.

Lord Garrick, once her enemy and now one of her most trusted advisors, stepped forward. His mechanical arm whirred softly as he gestured to the southern territories. "The giants appear to be following ley lines – the same paths the wild magic favors. They're not just destroying villages; they're... corrupting the land itself."

"Like a poison in the veins of Aethoria," Mira added from her place among the Keepers. The young mage had grown into her power and position, though her face still carried the wonder of one who would never take magic for granted. "The affected areas show signs of magical decay we haven't seen since..."

"Since Calidus." Lyra finished the thought. A chill ran through the room at the name. "Could he have survived somehow? Found his way back from wherever I sent him?"

"No." The voice came from the doorway, surprising them all. King Aldric entered, leaning on a staff carved from heart-wood. "This is something older than Calidus. Something that should have remained buried."

Lyra studied her father's face, noting new lines of worry. "You know what these things are."

It wasn't a question. Aldric nodded slowly. "There are secrets in the old histories. Things I should have told you long ago." He moved to the table, hands tracing patterns on the map that made the magical displays flicker. "The shadow giants aren't invaders – they're guardians. Corrupted ones."

"Guardians of what?" Darius asked, though his tone suggested he already feared the answer.

"Of boundaries," Aldric replied. "Not just between nations, but between realities. The wild magic's awakening didn't just change our world – it weakened the walls between worlds. And there are things in the spaces between that hunger for what we have here."

Silence fell over the war room as the implications sank in. Lyra felt Aurora stir in Darius's arms, the baby's magic reaching out to brush against her own – a reminder of everything they had to lose.

"How do we fight them?" she asked finally.

"Not with steel or spells." Aldric's eyes found the Crown of Whispers. "The giants were created by the first rulers of Aethoria – your ancestors. Their power flows in your veins, in Aurora's. But using it... there would be a price."

"There's always a price." Lyra's voice was steady. "Name it."

"Lyra—" Darius started, but she silenced him with a look.

"I chose this," she said softly. "All of it. The crown, the kingdom, the consequences. Whatever comes next, I'll face it."

She turned back to the council, voice ringing with authority. "Mira, gather the Keepers. We need to understand exactly how these giants are corrupting the ley lines. Lord Garrick, mobilize the army – not to fight, but to evacuate anyone in the giants' path. Aren, I want our fastest riders spreading the word to every settlement from here to the southern sea."

As the council members rushed to carry out her orders, Lyra felt Darius's free hand find hers. She squeezed it, drawing strength from his touch.

"I'm coming with you," he said quietly.

"I know." She managed a small smile. "You always do."

Aurora cooed, a sound like windchimes, and the air around them shimmered with possibilities. For a moment, Lyra saw echoes of other paths – lives where she'd never found the crown, never led a rebellion, never loved a man who'd crossed battle lines to stand beside her. But those were shadows. This was her reality, her responsibility, her choice.

The Crown of Whispers pulsed gently, resonating with the wild magic flowing through Aethoria's veins—her veins, her daughter's.

"Together then," she said, as much to herself as to Darius. "One last time."

But even as she spoke the words, something deeper whispered that this was not an ending but a beginning. The next chapter in a story that had been writing itself since the first rulers of Aethoria drew power from the land itself.

As the sun rose fully over her changed kingdom, Lyra Valenwood – rebel, queen, mother, guardian – prepared to write her own page in that ancient tale.

Whatever the cost, whatever the consequence, she would keep her people safe. She would keep her daughter's future bright. She would keep Aethoria free.

The next great adventure was about to begin.

The End

NOTE FROM THE AUTHOR

Dear Fellow Wanderer,

You have walked with me through the enchanted realms of Aethoria, witnessed battles woven with magic and steel, and shared in Lyra's journey from rebel to queen. For this, you have my deepest gratitude.

If this tale has kindled a spark of wonder in your heart, I ask you to share that magic with others seeking their next adventure. Your words, like whispers carried on the wind, can guide fellow readers to these pages. A few moments of your time could illuminate the path for countless others.

Share your thoughts in the Scrolls of Memory:

📚 The Grand Archive (Amazon)
⭐ The Chronicles of Readership (Goodreads)

Should you wish to stay connected to this realm:

- Join the Fellowship: Sign up for magical updates at *RavenFontaine.com/Newsletter-Signup/*
- Explore hidden treasures: Visit my writing sanctuary at *RavenFontaine.com*

Your journey through these pages has meant more than you know. Every review shared, every word written, helps this story find its way to those who need it most.

Until our paths cross again in the realms of story,

Raven Fontaine
Keeper of Tales

ABOUT THE AUTHOR

Raven Fontaine is an author who breathes life into epic fantasy worlds filled with rich characters, powerful magic, and slow-burn romances that leave readers captivated. Raven's work delves into the complexities of love, power, and identity, exploring how people survive and grow in dystopian and fantastical settings. With a background in mythology and folklore, Raven expertly blends ancient legends with modern themes, creating immersive stories where the stakes are high and emotions run deep.

Growing up surrounded by books, Raven developed a passion for storytelling early on, drawing inspiration from classic fantasy, historical epics, and romantic adventures. Raven's fascination with the tension between power and vulnerability, destiny and choice, drives much of the conflict in their novels. When not writing, Raven is often traveling, exploring forgotten ruins, or getting lost in nature, always seeking new sources of inspiration for the next great adventure.

Whether exploring distant lands or crafting intricate plots, Raven Fontaine is committed to creating stories that resonate with readers long after they turn the final page.

ALSO BY RAVEN FONTAINE

RAVEN FONTAINE
SOVEREIGN HEARTS

9 798899 653053